CORPSE
and
ROBBERS

CORPSE
and
ROBBERS

Douglas and Dorothy
STAPLETON

COACHWHIP PUBLICATIONS
Greenville, Ohio

To M. M. Hill

*whose constant prodding made the writing
of this book not only possible but necessary.*

Corpse and Robbers, by Douglas and Dorothy Stapleton
© 2023 Coachwhip Publications edition

First published 1954
Douglas Stapleton, 1907-1972
Dorothy Stapleton, 1917-1970
CoachwhipBooks.com

ISBN 1-61646-554-9
ISBN-13 978-1-61646-554-4

1

Miss Emily was formidable even as she went down under the blow. Her very bulk and solidity shook her big comfortable old house to its foundations, rattling her Spode in the pine corner cupboard and threatening the very existence of the Sevres figurines on her living room mantel. Even in defeat she went down magnificently, like a great tree crashing and shuddering to earth. With stunned incomprehension she sat spraddle-legged on her best summer grass rug, propped half erect on stout trunklike arms while pinwheels of light swirled giddily across the dark. She shook her metal-curlered head clankingly, and her vision cleared.

The front door was closing.

"I've been clobbered," stated Miss Emily in a voice tinged less with anger than with awe at the audacity of anyone daring to touch the person of Miss Emily. With the full realization of this indignity Miss Emily cut loose, violence and volume making up for a manifest inaccuracy.

"Murder! I've been murdered!"

It sounded boomingly satisfactory in Miss Emily's still ringing ears, so she bellowed again, "I've been murdered!"

It is not true that Miss Emily's second bellow cracked the huge picture window Jake Scudder had ill-advisedly set in the old Foster house across the street, though Miss Thalia Marsten, Miss Emily's neighbor to the rear, enjoyed relating the story. Miss Thalia didn't like the picture window and she didn't like Jake. Nor is it true that Miss Emily's voice was heard down at 19th Street—a matter of forty-odd blocks—and brought out the police, the fire department and the rescue squad.

At Miss Emily's third and, some say, most stentorian bellow, lights flicked on, and Cassie, her ebony complexion fear-bleached to a blonde mahogany, rumped her way through the swinging door, a poker in one massive hand and a formidable but rusty six-shooter in the other. She looked down at Miss Emily spraddle-legged on the floor.

"You kilt?"

Miss Emily took swift inventory before looking up. "Don't be a fool, Cassie."

"Then who you kilt?" Cassie's color was returning as she peered around the living room. "Miss Emily, I don't see no corpse."

"He got away. And put down that blunderbuss, Cassie. It might go off and kill somebody."

For easier identification Cassie waggled the six-shooter at Miss Emily. "This here?"

"And the way you're waving it around, it's likely to be me. Put that thing down!" Even from the floor Miss Emily had a commanding presence.

Cassie gazed uncertainly down at Miss Emily. "You *sure* you ain't kilt? Or mebbe shot fatally dead?"

For the first time since her ignominious clobbering Miss Emily took serious stock of her person, from her man-sized terry-cloth scuffs—one of which she discovered was missing—to her broad and mannish shoulders. "Got all my parts." She shifted her weight to one arm and put her freed hand to the sternly ordered ridges of her metal curlers and pressed gingerly.

Miss Emily swore loudly, violently and fluently while Cassie's uneasy smile broadened slowly into relief, widened to admiration and then slit her face with a grin of awed fascination.

"I sure am glad you ain't hurt."

"Hurt?" Miss Emily roared. "Hurt? I'm murdered. Assassinated!" Her deep voice dropped to a chuckle. "Help me up." Miss Emily extended her hand and Cassie reached for it.

"Don't anybody move!" The command came from the darkened porch.

Cassie shrieked like a calliope robbed of its young and flung herself on Miss Emily protectively. "He come back!"

With some difficult Miss Emily untangled herself. "Don't be an idiot. It's the police."

A lean, lanky and serious-looking young man stood in the doorway, thrusting his State Trooper's broad-brimmed hat back with the barrel of his service pistol. He holstered the gun and helped Miss Emily to her feet while Cassie scrambled to dubious protection behind a ladder-back chair. The young man grinned. "Who won that fall?"

Miss Emily shook herself into the folds of a gray flannel wrapper and glared at him. "Someone broke in and attacked me."

"Attacked you?" The young man stared for a moment at Miss Emily's capable bulk and finally nodded. "Okay. Where's the body?"

At this second tribute to her indestructibility Miss Emily blinked, then eyed the Trooper sternly. "Impudent puppy, aren't you?" She grimaced ruefully. "Got away. Clobbered me and got away. In the dark."

Without wasting further questions the trooper called over his shoulder, "Search the grounds and pick up anyone you see." He turned back to Miss Emily. "Any description?" He edited that after one glance at Miss Emily's face. "I suppose not."

Whatever else he might have said was drowned out in the combined shrieks of fire and ambulance sirens disputing for right-of-way on the narrow side street.

From the melee Dr. Walter Dolman emerged with such monumental dignity that Miss Emily said of him afterward, "He's just the sort of man you'd invite to an earthquake, if you were planning to have an earthquake."

At that time, however, her comments on his medical skill, education and ancestors were unprintable, especially after he had removed her metal curlers, poked at her scalp and clucked happily. "No abrasions. But you'd better come down to the hospital tomorrow for a check-up. Could be concussion. Take two of these pills and lie down."

Such calmness left Miss Emily so astonished that she actually took the pills. Nothing, however, could have made her lie down while there were noises going on in her house. As soon as the doctor had left she was up and thudding her walking stick down the hall to the living room, her flannel robe clutched tight around her, her iron-gray hair in wild disarray from the recent removal of her curlers.

The State Trooper was opening drawers under the stern inspection of Cassie.

"He isn't going to steal the silver, Cassie."

"That your great-granddaddy's silver," Cassie commented darkly, as if that made it especially vulnerable.

The trooper grinned, shoved the drawer closed with his hip and slouched against the table. "I'm Don Corley. Sergeant Don Corley."

Miss Emily nodded. "Knew your father. Best plumber I ever knew. Why aren't you a plumber? We need some good ones."

Don grinned. "I'm studying law."

Miss Emily glanced up and down his trim uniform. "And practicing it on the side? Studying nights?"

"Daytime. Policemen work at night." Miss Emily maneuvered her bulk into a chair and rested her hands on the silver knob of her stick. "Take that chair over there. They tell me George Washington used to sprawl in it, and you're just about as lanky and disjointed as he was."

Don grinned and accepted the chair. To Cassie, the seating of Trooper Corley in Miss Emily's presence automatically made him a guest and, as such, he was to be treated with respect and Miss Emily's famous coffee.

Don settled into his chair. "I hope it was a burglar." At Miss Emily's startled "Hope?" he went on, "And not something worse."

"Oh!"

"You probably walked in just as he got started. What made you get up? Hear a noise?"

Miss Emily glanced down her bulk and sighed. "When you're as big as I am, you need a lot of fuel. I got up for a snack."

She grinned at Don. "Did you find the weapon? What was it. A sashweight?"

"You won't like this." Don smiled and held up a pencil thrust into the neck of a bottle.

"A coke bottle!" Miss Emily snorted fiercely. "A coke bottle! Of all the impudent, impertinent—"

"You could have been hurt badly."

"A coke bottle!" The indignity of it swamped Miss Emily. "Clobbered by a coke bottle."

"Do you drink cokes?"

Miss Emily rumbled violently as if she considered herself criticized. "Everybody drinks cokes."

"What I meant was, could the intruder have just grabbed one—or did he bring it with him?"

"They're all over the place." Suddenly the ignominy of it hit her again. She thumped her stick violently. "Clobbered by a coke bottle! If I'd had this stick . . ." Miss

Emily swooshed it past Don's head and then held it rigid, pointing. "Did you do that?"

Don swiveled to follow the pointing of Miss Emily's rock-like arm. There was a desk, its flap open, several papers scattered across its green baize surface. He shook his head. "Didn't touch it." He set the bottle down carefully and started for the desk. "Is something wrong with it?"

"I may be casual but I'm not sloppy." Miss Emily heaved herself to her feet and hurtled past him to brake herself to a skidding halt with her stick. Her eyes rapidly scanned the desk.

"Anything missing?" Don stooped to peer into pigeonholes.

Miss Emily scowled. "Nothing but my unanswered mail is disturbed." She frowned down at the papers scattered across the desk. "Maybe I do take a little long to answer my mail, but I didn't think anyone would get impatient enough to come after it."

Don picked up a penholder and, one by one, flipped over the unanswered mail, most of it gaudy postcards, nine of them of the Azalea Gardens in Charleston. "You fond of azaleas?"

Miss Emily grunted ferociously. "This is vacation time and everybody who goes to Charleston sends me pictures of the Azalea Gardens. Last year I got twenty-six. Only ten so far this summer."

"Ten?" Don hastily checked them over. "I count only nine." He peered under the desk and squinted behind it.

Miss Emily arranged the nine identical cards in rows and studied them dubiously. "Pretty awful, aren't they? Dead and stuffed. And the gardens really are beautiful." She flicked them over, reciting, "Martha . . . Jane . . . Eloise . . . Candy . . . Billie—I know sixteen Billies . . . Dottie—I'd recognize that backhand anywhere . . . S&S—

that's Sam and Sarah . . . Agnes—no mistaking that blunt hand . . . Arthur—Jane's son."

"Can you figure out what's missing?"

Miss Emily's blunt finger tapped each of the nine varied scrawls. She frowned thoughtfully. "Squiggles is missing."

"Squiggles? Is anybody really named Squiggles?"

"Called it Squiggles because the signature started with M-squiggle-squiggle-big squiggle-squiggle. I have dozens of friends in Charleston whose names start with M and fully half of them are stupid enough to have written like that."

Don glanced down the nine inane vacation messages. "Couldn't you tell from the message who it was from?"

Miss Emily snorted. "Anybody who signs M-squiggle-squiggle can't write a message you could read and hasn't brains enough to make sense if you could read it. And anyway, I'm not interested in who it's from. I want to know where it has gone."

Don glared down at the nine cards, tapping them irritably. "That's important, of course. But I'd like to know *why* it's gone."

Miss Emily looked up at him, her fine old eyes squinting with new respect. "Don, I think maybe you'll make a good policeman—and a better lawyer."

At that moment what appeared to be a blue-and-gold pinwheel on fire burst through Miss Emily's front door and catapulted into the living room. Don Corley whirled and grabbed for his pistol only to find his arm pinned by a stick in Miss Emily's hand.

"Don't be an idiot. That's only Carol-Ann. She often comes in like that." Miss Emily sighed. "Especially when she's mad."

2

Carol-Ann wasn't mad. She was having the time of her young life. It wasn't often she had an opportunity to throw a tantrum and, having that sort of red hair, she dearly loved throwing tantrums.

Two Troopers, one on either side of her, looked like men who wished wholeheartedly they had taken up ditch-digging and stuck with it. One of them released her warily, wiping his face with the back of his hand. "We caught this trespasser hiding behind the . . ." He gaped, stared at his partner, who finished for him . . . "the hydrangea."

Carol-Ann swept her other arm free and as the two Troopers winced, blurted out, "It isn't hydrangea. It's forsythia. And I wasn't hiding. I was bringing Miss Emily some jellied consommé." She shook out the voluminous sleeve of the blue-and-gold kimono and revealed a fragile bowl in which quivered a ruddy, gelatinous mass. She stared at it scornfully. "No one but Cynthia Scudder would think of consommé at a time like this." Very deliberately she tilted her hand and, before either of the sweating Troopers could grab it, the bowl slid, teetered and shattered into a glutinous puddle. From her neat pretense of wrath she turned a sweet, forgiving smile on one of the men. "Now see what you made me do. And that was dear Cynthia's very best Haviland."

The Trooper appealed to the room helplessly. "I didn't! I never touched . . . Look, she hung on to that bowl till . . . She done it herself." Carol-Ann could feel the bewildered reproach in his glance. "A lady wouldn't a done that."

"On the contrary." The slow deliberateness of Don's words brought Carol-Ann's eyes around. She pretended she saw him for the first time slouched wearily against the desk. He sighed, waving the men away. "Only a lady would dare do a thing like that. And Miss Foster is very much a lady. Get back outside."

"You!" Carol-Ann stormed across at Don, just as if she hadn't known he was there before she ever let the Troopers find her. "Did you order these goons to arrest me? Why, you . . . you . . . YOU!"

She watched Don's slow flush. "Don't call my men goons or I'll forget you're a lady and . . ."

"Seein' as you two are old friends," the older Trooper interrupted tactfully, "we'll leave her with you."

Carol-Ann ignored their departure, stabbing the buckle of Don's belt with a stiff forefinger. Since he didn't seem to be taking any decisive action she goaded him. "And you'll what?"

"He could start with a spanking," suggested Miss Emily. Carol-Ann turned to see her leaning on her stick and watching them with pleased expectancy.

"That should have been retroactive." Don said it firmly, and Carol-Ann turned in time to see his scowl replaced by a tired grin. "By at least fifteen years."

Carol-Ann wrapped herself in dignity and the blue-and-gold kimono. "You don't even know what I was like fifteen years ago!" She shook a challenging finger at him, but the effectiveness was lost in the folds of the kimono sleeve. She thrust it back and started again, aware that her arm looked very nice and brown against the deep blue.

She kept her finger rigid and uncompromising. "You don't even know . . ."

Don studied the finger under his nose until he was almost cross-eyed. He seemed, in fact, to talk to the finger instead of to Carol-Ann. "You were eight years old, in the third grade in Miss Willet's class, and your knees were knobby." He turned to go.

Carol-Ann saw him stoop to pick up a coke bottle. He was actually leaving!

Don straightened, shaking the bottle at her. "And you shot spitballs through the fifth grade window with rubber bands." He peered at her across the upraised coke bottle, pleasantly close. "I suspect you took 'em off your pigtails. The rubber bands, I mean."

"They were not pigtails." Carol-Ann reached out to grab the coke bottle by its neck and felt Don's hand close with alarming firmness over her wrist.

His voice, however, was surprisingly calm. "That was evidence." Carol-Ann loosened her grip and watched miserably as Don stalked to the door, bottle held aloft like a torch, mouth and eyes grim. He turned and looked back. "Miss Foster, I'll have to ask you to report to headquarters for fingerprinting. So we can identify and eliminate yours from this—" he shook the coke bottle menacingly—"this weapon."

Carol-Ann gasped and started after him. She stamped her foot, glaring down at the puddle and considering the advisability of kicking jellied consommé around Miss Emily's living room.

"Don't!" Miss Emily ordered peremptorily. "And besides, you did wear pigtails."

"Of course I did. And I shot spitballs into the fifth grade room, too. But imagine that Thing remembering."

"Maybe he was in the fifth grade room."

"Naturally. Why do you think I shot spitballs at it?"

"Oh!" Miss Emily massaged several of her chins with the silver knob of her stick, her grim old eyes lighting. "You were in love with him."

Carol-Ann nodded miserably. "Of course. And he's such a goop. Worse than that, he's a snob."

"Don Corley? A snob?" This time the surprise in Miss Emily's eyes was genuine. "What's Don got to be a snob about? The Corleys were good plain people, but—"

Carol-Ann stirred the jellied consommé with her toe. "He's a snob about me. Because I'm a lady—a Foster—F.F.V." Carol-Ann abandoned the consommé and marched on Miss Emily belligerently. "When I was eight years old he used to address me as 'Miss Foster.' 'Miss!' Even then he used to say I was a lady. Don't you think I got tired of it?"

Carol-Ann banged both fists against Miss Emily's vast bosom. "Darn it, I want him to think of me as a woman."

"Then keep throwing spitballs," Miss Emily counselled, and stepped away from Carol-Ann's pummeling. "And you don't have to batter me. I've been battered."

Carol-Ann was instantly contrite. "Oh, I'm a horrible beast!" She convoyed Miss Emily to her chair just as Cassie lumbered through the swinging door, her broad hip bumping it aside to make way for a large tray amply spread.

Cassie spotted the gooey mess on the floor and slid the tray hurriedly on to the table. She shot Miss Emily a worried look. "You feel all right? For sure? Even with your brains beat out?"

Carol-Ann stared coldly down at the mess. "That is consommé that my dear Mrs. Jake Scudder sent over. With the hope, of course, that Miss Emily would personally return such a lovely bowl." She nudged the shattered Haviland with her toe. "Unfortunately it's broken."

Cassie's dark face registered amazement. "She 'spect Miss Emily gonna pussonally return a bowl she sent over? That woman is jest' po' white trash."

"That woman," Carol-Ann explained, "is very rich white trash."

Cassie shook her head. "There is po' white trash and mebbe there is rich white trash, but that woman is jes' po' white trash with money."

"Cassie," Carol-Ann smiled delightedly, "you are speaking of my bread and butter."

"That woman ain't nobody's bread and butter. She's pickles and vinegar. How come you work for her? A lady like you . . ."

Carol-Ann winced. "Cassie, even Fosters like to eat. It's a habit I got into when very young."

Miss Emily, who had started in on cold chicken, waved a swiftly denuded bone at Carol-Ann. "You get plenty of rent for that house."

Carol-Ann grimaced. "My employment as Cynthia Scudder's secretary was part of the conditions of that very nice rent. Needless to say, the condition was made before I met dear Cynthia." She thought that over and added, in all fairness, "Or before dear Cynthia had seen the Foster ancestral home."

Miss Emily looked up. "Fiddlesticks! Ancestral home. It's one old Judge Marsten stuck your daddy with less than fifty years ago. It's a monstrosity."

"Dear Cynthia thinks it's quaint." Carol-Ann puckered her eyes, pursed her mouth, and quirked her head in a silly, birdlike motion that cruelly caricatured Cynthia Scudder's efforts to be ladylike. "So officially it is now quaint."

"And those picture windows! Makes it look like a horse in a petticoat." Miss Emily lifted one corner of her monumental sandwich, peered in and nodded. "Why'd you let her put 'em in?"

"It was in the contract," Carol-Ann quoted mechanically. "'To improve said property at the tenant's desire and expense.' Jake's a stickler for contracts."

"But you don't have to work for that woman!"

"Jake demands the letter of the contract, and he specified I should act as his wife's social secretary. So I do." She shrugged. "I don't really mind. And it's only for a couple more weeks. Until the Scudders move to the old Beauregard Tayloe place."

"That's one good thing the Scudders have done. Now Judge Bo can have his dream house, electric kitchen and all. But I shudder to think of what the Scudders will do in restoring Holley Hall."

"Judge Bo is supervising that—step by step. And I wish he wouldn't be so meticulous. He's holding things up. The Scudders should have moved last week and I could have quit being a social secretary. Of course, you couldn't call Cynthia very social, and she needs a secretary like I need a third leg. Anyway, sometimes I even like the old pirate."

"Pirate?"

"Jake. At least he's an honest old pirate. No, that isn't what I mean. I mean, he's honestly an old pirate. He admits he fought and robbed and bribed his way to the top. He's even frank about buying Cynthia's way into Virginia society. If it's something she wants, get it for her."

"He'll never make it." Miss Emily reached for another slice of ham, halted momentarily at Cassie's scowl and then refused to be intimidated.

"Jake thinks he will. And Cynthia's making the big step tomorrow. He's gotten her nominated Chairman of the Marsten Memorial Fund." Carol-Ann whipped her hand to her mouth. "Oh! That was supposed to be a secret."

"Bosh!" Miss Emily munched and swallowed. "Everybody in town knows it. Only I can't think why Thalia Marsten would allow it. She hates the Scudders—or says she does."

Carol-Ann frowned at her mules. "Jake gave the land and he's donating a big hunk of money."

"The way Thalia makes a tin god out of that old reprobate father of hers, money isn't enough. Or maybe it is. She's been working on that memorial for years. Maybe Jake's gifts weakened her."

Carol-Ann shook her head. "I don't know how he got around her pride, but he did. He's sure of it, and been sure for at least two weeks. So sure he gloats."

Miss Emily glowered. "And who wants a memorial to that old skinflint anyway?"

Carol-Ann shrugged. "Miss Thalia. Judge Theodore Clayton Marsten founded Virginia Beach."

"Founded fiddlesticks! His granddaddy bought up about four miles of sand to raise oranges on, only they wouldn't grow here, which he should have known. All old Theodore did was sell his granddaddy's land to a syndicate and get rich. And died poor from the unalterable conviction that the way to make money was to buy stock at one hundred and sell it at ninety."

Carol-Ann giggled. "He didn't."

"Well, he may not have meant to," Miss Emily conceded, "but that's what happened. He had either the worst luck or the poorest judgment—or both—of any human being I ever saw." She sighed gustily. "Even so, I suppose I'll go to Thalia's fund-raising party tomorrow." Miss Emily put a hand up to her straggling hair. "And me with a headache and no hair-set."

"Oh!" Carol-Ann leapt to her feet and started for the door. "I'm sorry. I shouldn't have kept you up, after what happened. Good night. I'll—"

Miss Thalia Marsten scuttled through the kitchen door, peering behind her. "Men! Men! That Dan Corley! The idea of telling me he was patrolling the grounds! Why, I can remember when he was a little snip in the fifth grade." She snapped a bright and artificially toothy smile at Carol-Ann and Miss Emily. "Of course, I was just a child myself. Patrolling! He sneaked around that bush at me." She peered through the glass of the front door, tugging aside the curtain conspiratorially. She straightened her gaunt body and shook her head ominously at Miss Emily. "He's still there. I tell you, the police in this town are terribly lax. Father would never have stood for it. Never around until after something happens."

Miss Emily sighed wearily. "Thalia, will you quit talking long enough to say something?"

Miss Thalia gasped, her long, bony face puckering into a threat of tears. "I just came over to see how you were. After all, we are old friends and I should think old friends could be old . . ." Miss Thalia, hopelessly entangled in that sentence, brushed it aside with thin, fluttering hands and rushed into another. "At least you don't seem badly hurt, Emily, and I will say it's a mercy you were wearing your heavy curlers. No telling what might have happened. . . ." Miss Thalia paused expectantly. Nothing was forthcoming, and Miss Thalia looked briefly hurt, but she managed to stir up her own excitement. "Are you coming to the Memorial Party to dear Father?" She bugged her eyes at Miss Emily without waiting for a reply. "Do you think you can make it? Really, Emily, I wouldn't want you to miss it, even if you came in a bandage."

"I shall be adequately clothed, Thalia."

But Miss Thalia was off in dimensions of her own. "It's going to be such a beautiful affair. And I shall be both sad and happy, proud and humble, elated and downcast. All those distinguished people gathered to honor dear Father. In a sylvan glade, under stately trees, a monument shall rise. His illustrious name shall be emblazoned. . . ." She sighed. "What a pity young Ted won't be there. He would have loved it so. He was devoted to Father." She came back to reality with a start. "Oh, I'd better get home. I must get my beauty sleep. You don't have to see me home. I'll just skip out the back way. . . ."

Carol-Ann, hearing the back door close on Miss Thalia, turned to Miss Emily in puzzlement. "Who is young Ted?"

"Young Ted," Miss Emily explained, "is now nearing sixty."

"Oh! Mister Theo, the Bouncing Bachelor." Carol-Ann identified him in terms of her own generation. "When did he die?"

"He's not dead. That's just Thalia's way of talking. He's very lively and he'd just as soon attend a Memorial Party to the Judge as he would a cannibal feast—as the main dish. He hated the old tyrant and felt the only smart thing his father ever did was die and leave him his real estate. Thalia got the cash—what there was left after the Judge's speculations. No, Ted's probably gone off up the Chesapeake in that lugger of his. He does it every now and then. It's his only escape from Thalia when she starts waving the old Judge's bones. I can imagine what she's been like ever since this confounded Memorial was actually proposed."

"I'm afraid I proposed it." Carol-Ann took the blame. "When Jake was looking for something to give to the town—a sort of gesture of good will—I suggested the Memorial. The idea's been kicking around so long . . ." Carol-Ann defended herself against Miss Emily's scowl. "I really thought he meant it as a gesture of good will." Carol-Ann edged toward the door. "I really should be going. I'll just . . ."

"One minute." Cassie's ample form barred the door.

She swept aside her dressing gown in a dramatic gesture, revealing the poker, a skewer and Miss Emily's best bone-handled carving knife tucked into an improvised belt. "It'll be all right, if'n you take this." And she thrust the carving knife into Carol-Ann's unwilling hands.

Cassie, however, lacked the gift of prophecy.

3

Carol-Ann felt rakish and piratical as she slid out of Miss Emily's fanlight door and down the steps. Briefly she considered clutching the knife between her teeth and skulking through the dark. "Only I'm not sure I know how to skulk," she told herself, and giggled.

The giggle ended in a hiccoughing sigh that was trying to be a scream. A tall, menacing shadow had detached itself from the clump of forsythia and was starting toward her purposefully, unhurriedly. Carol-Ann stopped, backed up slowly, feeling the uneven bricks with horrible distinctness under the thin soles of her mules. Her hand came up, the knife flashing. If that lump in her throat would just turn into a good, lusty yell, but it blocked even breathing. And still the figure came on, slowly, inexorably.

For the first time the reality of tonight's adventure hit her. There had been a real intruder. She tried once more to scream. The lump moved a little, gave somewhere, and she whispered huskily, "I'll scream."

"Good idea, Miss Foster." Don's voice came matter-of-factly from the hulking figure, and somehow, in that instant, it was no longer hulking, but straight, tall and broad-shouldered.

"Oh—Don." Low, soft, tremulous. Carol-Ann, as if listening to herself with one ear, realized she couldn't have done it better if she had rehearsed it. In two words she had expressed release from fear, womanly dependence, admiration for his strength and gratitude for his protecting presence. It was good. She knew it was good. But it seemed to have no effect on that—that policeman.

"It's a good idea to scream if you think somebody is about to attack you—especially at almost three in the morning." He was beside her, reaching out for her wrist. "But that's no way to hold a knife. Not with your hand up and the point down. The attacker can see it and take it away from you. Like this."

Very deftly he squeezed her wrist and the knife dropped into his other hand. He took her arm and started her forward again, toward the lighted windows of the Foster house. No, now it was the Scudder house. And he kept talking.

"If you're going to use a knife, the best way is like this." He reached across her and picked up her limp right hand, pressing the bone handle into it, curling her fingers around it, point out and up. "There. It's much easier to slash up. And there's less defense against it. Also, you're more likely to hit a vital organ instead of just nicking a collarbone."

They were almost abreast of one of dear Cynthia's picture windows, and through the half drawn drapes Carol-Ann could see Jake Scudder's round, red face, redder now and mottled. He was shaking his fist at someone and shouting.

Don was still propelling her gently toward the house and, as they moved, the angle of vision changed. Cynthia was standing across the desk, her chiseled features hardened and twisting into a sneer. Behind her, slumped in a chair and peering up at her, was Andy, her brother. He shot a brief sneer at Jake and then turned his face back to Cynthia.

A few words did filter through the glass, ugly and vulgar. Carol-Ann could feel Don stiffen, felt, rather than saw him shake his head disapprovingly. "A gentleman shouldn't say things like that."

For the first time since Don had emerged from the shadows Carol-Ann got her voice back and working without lumps. "Don't you ever quit worrying about what a gentleman would do and think about what a MAN would do?"

For a long moment he looked down at her, the blunt angles and lean planes of his face accented and sculptured by the light from the window. Very slowly he reached out and caught her shoulders, pulled her close. There was, Carol-Ann realized, ample time for her to pull away. He pulled her closer, up on to her toes.

"I've often thought of it, ma'am."

He kissed her, long, hard, breathlessly. Her hand opened and the knife clattered to the brick walk. Long before she was ready for it he pushed her away. The angry stubbornness in the lines of his face had somehow miraculously dissolved, and he was grinning. "Under the circumstances, Miss Foster, that's what I think a man would do."

He stooped, picked up the knife and tucked it once more into her hand before he melted away into the shadows.

Ronnie Parker, Jake's nephew, was reaching for the knob as she entered. He looked at her for a long moment, and one eyebrow rose slowly and his mouth quirked. He leaned forward to peer over her shoulder into the night. "Isn't it dangerous being out at this hour?" His quirk became a grin.

Carol-Ann answered it with another. "Not now. The police seem to have things well in hand."

"Most efficient of them." He pushed the door shut, his arm sliding easily over her head, his grin tilted down. "My car will be safe on the street, then. Our Andy has, in his usual charming way, hogged the drive. Good night." He twinkled at her once more and strode off down the hall, a long-legged tweedy figure fading into the gloom.

Carol-Ann headed for her own apartment over the attached garage, when the quarrel seemed to break out again. Jake's voice rumbled out, from behind the sliding doors in what had been her father's den. Now it was Jake's combination den and office. It was furnished with deep leather chairs, a massive but practical desk and the undisguised rigidity of metal file cabinets. Despite its ruggedness Carol-Ann preferred it to what Cynthia had done to the rest of the house in her frantic efforts at "restoration."

Carol-Ann was passing the double doors when Cynthia slid open one panel. With the light behind her it was difficult to make out her expression but Carol-Ann was sure it was still twisted in anger, probably because of the tenseness of her long, svelte body.

From the room Carol-Ann heard Jake's voice, hoarse, angry, pitched to give orders distinctly and make them final. "And you'll get out and get a job or get out. I'm sick and tired of your sponging on your sister."

"Maybe you'd better ask my sister." Andy's voice was sulkily insolent. He raised it to carry across the room. "How about it, Sis?"

"Andy!" There was a momentary touch of panic in Cynthia's voice; then her own brand of command took over, high, sharp and brittle. "Jake! She's back. Miss Carol-Ann. . . ."

However inept the phrasing, it silenced Jake momentarily. Then his voice boomed out with conscious joviality, "Come in. Come in."

As Carol-Ann entered, Cynthia slithered to one side, still clutching the edge of the door with a white-knuckled hand. Andy seized the moment to slide over the arm of his chair and slouch out of the bright arc of light from the desk lamp. He shouldered his way past Carol-Ann without his usual smirk. His habitual sneer was replaced by a sullen droop and the padded arrogance of his shoulders had slumped ludicrously, giving him a shambling, hang-dog look. But there was nothing hangdog about the venom in his eyes. As he brushed past her, Cynthia reached out to touch his arm but he jerked petulantly away, glaring at her. Very low, intended only for Cynthia's ears, he aimed his words. "Fix it up, baby. And be sure you do. Or I'll kill the rat . . . and you wouldn't like that." He sneered and started on, then turned back. "Or would you?"

"I said get out!" Jake's voice cracked across the room and it was like a boot on Andy's trousers. He reared back defensively and lunged out the door, not looking back. Cynthia relaxed against the door with a shivering sigh.

Carol-Ann did her best to ignore Andy's exit. It wasn't difficult. She had had practice ignoring Andy. She stepped into the bright area of light and Jake peered at her across the desk, suddenly grinning. "Hi. How's the old girl? Not hurt bad, I hope. Though she'd boot my tail for even wishing her well." He chuckled, rubbing one hairy fist alongside his big nose. "I don't get much change outa Miss Emily."

At moments like this Carol-Ann almost liked Jake. He was big, lumbering, seemingly awkward and frankly common. She could even imagine Miss Emily liking him on his own earthy terms, if it hadn't been for Cynthia and her obsession with society. Carol-Ann was convinced she wouldn't like it, even if she could get in. The society Cynthia was aiming at would be too dull for so exotic and artificial a creature as Cynthia. Carol-Ann caught Jake's eye. He was studying the knife in her hand, amused.

"What a weapon! An outsized pig-sticker. If you figger you need that just to cross the street, Virginia Beach is in bad shape."

Carol-Ann laid the knife on the desk. "Cassie insisted on arming me. It's part of Miss Emily's best bone-handled carving set, so I must remember to return it."

"Miss Emily's carving set." Cynthia slid to the side of the desk and picked up the knife, turning it over and over in her hands. "Best bone-handled set, huh?" She flicked the knife back and forth under the desk lamp. "Looks kinda beat to me."

"It has taken four generations of carving to give it that 'kinda beat' look, Mrs. Scudder. And I'm sure Miss Emily prizes it. I'll return it tomorrow." Carol-Ann reached for the knife but Cynthia swished it away.

"No. It'll be a good excuse . . . I mean, I'll take it back and thank her for protecting you. And I can pick up my Haviland bowl at the same time."

"I'm afraid it got smashed."

"Smashed!" Cynthia's tone was incredulous and then skirled into high, brittle sharpness. "I paid twenty bucks for that thing just so I could send . . ." She pulled her voice down sharply at a gesture from Jake.

Carol-Ann nodded solemnly. *I know you bought that bowl just so you could send things around to correct old ladies so they'd think you had a complete set. It was a phony even if it was genuine—a come-on. If you'd had an honest set and honestly liked it I'd never have dropped it.* She didn't say that aloud. Instead she smiled at Jake. "Miss Emily isn't hurt, except for her dignity and her bottom. She sat down too hard."

Jake liked that. He chuckled. "They get the guy that done it?"

"He got away."

"Take anything?"

"The silliest thing. Just a postcard. Of the Azalea Gardens in Charleston."

Jake's smile flickered and died. He cut his eyes around to Cynthia, who was still dubiously examining the well-boned knife. He swung back to Carol, resuming his grin with an effort. "A postcard, huh? From Charleston?"

"Just one—and Miss Emily had dozens."

"Dozens?"

"Oh, she knows everybody in Charleston and they're always dropping her cards."

Jake relaxed, laughing. "Sure. I guess the old girl knows everybody who is anybody, all through the South."

Carol-Ann nodded, stifling a yawn. Three o'clock in the morning was late enough to be up. Cynthia laid the knife down with a tiny, metallic clatter. "I'll keep it here and return it in the morning. Good night."

"G'night. . . ." Jake's farewell was perfunctory.

Carol-Ann started down the hall, hearing Cynthia's high, insensitive voice gloating over the prospect of returning Miss Emily's knife—walking into Miss Emily's house.

Cynthia might be insensitive but Carol-Ann was not. The postcard from Charleston meant something to Jake—and it meant something to the intruder. It hadn't been a senseless, purposeless grab. She must remember to tell Don about it in the morning.

4

Carol-Ann looked up from her grapefruit as Ronnie, Jake's long and amiably strung together nephew, heaved himself up from the breakfast table, eyeing its overelegant, overelaborate settings. "It's pretty awful, isn't it? Even I can see that, and I'm just a mutt. Cynthia always overdoes things."

"Are you expressing an opinion or asking for a fight?"

Ronnie grinned down at her. "Loyal even unto Cynthia, eh? And belligerent, too. It comes of having red hair."

Carol-Ann started one hand toward her hair, as if to assure herself it was still there, then snatched it down, grinning. "I'm not going to fight with anybody. I feel too good today."

Ronnie's eyes twinkled at her. "Because a policeman kissed you last night?"

Carol-Ann gasped. "You—why, you couldn't see—I mean—"

Ronnie smirked. "I didn't need to. I saw your face when you came in. It had that I've-just-been-kissed look. And there were only policemen around."

"Can you deduce how unpopular you are at this moment?" Carol-Ann felt a little bewildered, rather than angry, as she would at anyone else, but Ronnie had a nonsensical manner that made even his impertinence amusing.

"I have the knack." Ronnie quirked a grin at her. "Right now I'm unpopular with my esteemed uncle, who is probably drawing up a new will, cutting me off with a dollar. It must get monotonous, cutting me off and putting me back in. He always does, you know. Put me back in, I mean." He studied the slim cylinder of his cigaret, scowling mildly. "I sometimes suspect he's fond of me, in his way. And I like the old boy. In my way, of course." He frowned slightly. "But why you stick around is more than I can see. And you don't have to be up at this ungodly hour. Cynthia won't stir before eleven."

Carol-Ann attacked her grapefruit again. "I like getting up early. Besides, I have a lot to do today. The Memorial Party . . ."

"That!" Ronnie glared at his cigaret and ground it out savagely. "I wish Uncle Jake hadn't . . ." Suddenly he grinned at her again. "My wishing that is why I'm in the doghouse right now. Well, so long. I'll be at the shindig, but meantime I've got to run."

Carol-Ann was busy for the next few hours, preparing for Cynthia's coming social triumph. Somehow Jake had managed to get Cynthia appointed as Chairman of the Marsten Memorial Fund Committee. Just how Carol-Ann hadn't had time to puzzle out either. Certainly money alone hadn't done it.

Cynthia glanced at the ormolu clock. It was time to get Cynthia started. Cynthia took time to get going, and Carol-Ann herself had to get dressed.

A few minutes and a shower later she surveyed herself in her mother's old pier-glass. The light cashmere sweater did very nice things to her figure and a moss-green skirt had a nice outdoorsy look, just suited to the afternoon party. She made a little face at the glass and started off after Cynthia.

At the open door Carol-Ann paused, seeing Cynthia at her best. Cynthia knew clothes and she knew she knew them. It made her superbly confident. Years as a model had given her poise and posture, stylized but suited to her slim, dramatic figure. Those same years had given her a knowledge of colors and materials. Jake's money had given her the opportunity to exercise those talents to the fullest.

She turned, preening before the triple mirror, stroking the sleek lines of the shocking-pink suit that set off so admirably her honey-gold hair. The wide dramatic flare of the revers proclaimed it a Jacques Fath original, and the flouncy peplum said very decided things about her slim hips. And only Mister Johns could have created that silly fragile hat in the precise shade of green to go with shocking-pink. For a breath-taking moment Carol-Ann felt envy for those lovely things. They were so beautifully right for Cynthia. And so wholly and completely wrong for Miss Thalia's garden party.

Cynthia pirouetted away from the mirror, her thin, almost classic face lighted with sheer animal pleasure. She waved gayly at Carol-Ann. "Come in! Come in, darling." Her voice was pitched high, thin with excitement.

"You're a knock-out, Sis." Andy sprawled back in a quilted slipper chair, noticed Carol-Ann and saluted with his cigaret. "Some babe, huh?"

It was said with magnificent self-satisfaction, as if he had personally invented her and arranged for the perpetual shower of Jake's money that made such splendor possible. "That's my Sis." He waved a sallow hand benignly. He was permanently sallow. Even his carefully acquired suntan looked unhealthy.

She swung her eyes back to the suit. "It's lovely." She tried to picture it among the tweeds and the light cotton prints of the Little Theater group. Unconsciously she shook her head.

"So it ain't right." Cynthia said it with bitter realization. "I mighta known." She flung Andy's feet to one side and slumped on the foot of the slipper chair.

"Aw, wear it. It's a whing-ding. And who says Miss Smarty-Pants knows?"

"I do." Jake's voice boomed behind Carol-Ann, making her jump. It also jerked Andy upright in the slipper chair. "And for you, Andy, that had better be as good as a written guarantee. If I say something, I mean it." He strode past Carol-Ann to stand over Andy. "And I back it up. Including what I said last night."

Cynthia threw out an arm between them. "Now, Jake . . ." Sudden fear showed in her eyes—but not fear of Jake. The fear was in her eyes when they rested on Andy, slouched and sullen on the slipper chair.

"Don't blow your stack." Andy started up, glowering. "I'm leaving."

Jake's big hand shoved him back. "You're staying. We're all going to this blowout. See? Like a family. We stand by Cyn. This here deal is important and nothing better happen to spoil it."

5

After some argument Carol-Ann had gotten Cynthia into a blue shantung, despite her horrified protests that she had worn it at least twice! Carol-Ann had stared at her. "How many times do you think I've worn this outfit?"

"I never noticed. But what difference does that make? I got plenty of clothes." Things like that endeared Cynthia to people.

It wasn't until they were headed for the much-publicized Memorial Party that Carol-Ann learned how much of that publicity Jake was responsible for. As he swept the big car into shaded Holly Drive he grinned at Cynthia. "This time it ain't gonna miss, baby. It's made. In the bag. It took finagling—and a little pressure. And dough. But I done it. And I wangled a deal with Movietone to cover it. And use it. You're gonna be sitting up there with the Missus Bigs and the Governor on every screen in the U.S.A."

Jake waved airily. "I hadda get Luke into this to get the Governor to come."

Cynthia fidgeted her shoulders petulantly. "Luke Snedicker! That creep should turn blue! Why-ja hafta . . ."

"Look!" Jake slowed the Cadillac so he could swing completely around. "Luke don't like this any more'n you like him. But he's in. I need him. So he stays in. Also, he's

my partner." The finality in Jake's voice penetrated even
to Cynthia.

"Andy's still with us." Jake paid this information no
heed and Cynthia shifted restlessly again. "But I notice . . ."
Cynthia had resumed her elegance, now tinged with contempt. "Ronnie couldn't make it."

Jake's big shoulders hunched defensively. "He hadda go
out early. But he promised he'd be there."

"He hadda go out early," Cynthia mimicked, and then
reverted to culture to give weight to her sarcasm. "I've
noticed the deah boy is getting out early these mornings.
And comes in late. Last night it was neally three." She
made that dig especially sweet and then dropped the culture. "What's he do? Keep a harem?"

"That's right." Jake said it so flatly it defied further
questioning and Cynthia sank back, and stared at the rusticity of Holly Drive.

To Carol-Ann this artfully maintained rusticity was one
of the pleasanter manifestations of the schizophrenia that
was Virginia Beach. It was not really an old town, though
the English had first set foot on American soil here.

The town itself was only a little over fifty years old,
started on Judge Marsten's land as a resort for the older
families of Richmond, Norfolk and Petersburg, by frenetic
developers who had skinned the land bare to build and
sell quickly. It was the earliest and most frenetic of these
developers that they were on their way to honor—Judge
Theodore Marsten.

In more recent years a calmer, saner breed had moved
in—men with money and plans, to build lavish hotels and
sprawling country clubs with championship golf courses
and, of course, real estate developments. These were men
who appreciated the cash value of the near-tropical trees
and had preserved them—at nice prices, of course.

The town was divided between the two factions—the Old Guard who had built their Victorian monstrosities and the newer moneyed crowd who, having footed some fantastic bills, felt that the town was theirs. There was still another element, Army and Navy families of upper rank, who moved in and out with that curious mixture of permanence and detachment that only upper bracket brass can achieve.

Carol-Ann knew these three elements would meet—and quite possibly clash—at Miss Thalia's Memorial Party, and she didn't relish the thought. Add to that the mysterious undercurrent of force Jake was applying to get Cynthia accepted by the Old Guard and you had an explosive mixture. *If I only knew where he was applying pressure, I might be able to spot incipient outbreaks and do something to prevent a real explosion. But I don't know. Jake's been too secretive. I'm not looking forward to this at all. Not at all.*

Cynthia's hand closed convulsively around her wrist, startling her. "I'm scared!" For an instant Carol-Ann Eked her for this one genuine display of normal reaction. She patted the thin gloved hand on her arm.

"There's nothing to be afraid of. Just a bunch of old women in frumpy dresses having a big time."

As they approached the site for the Theodore Clayton Marsten Memorial Little Theater, State Troopers were trying to direct traffic. Carol-Ann found herself scanning the roadsides, looking for Don. She thought she saw him but he was too far off in a tangle of cars to make even the most unladylike halloo practical. But he was around. She settled back in the seat and let Jake pick his way among the cars and find a parking spot.

"Get out and open the door for me," Cynthia smirked. "The way a gentleman oughta."

"Huh?" Jake swiveled from his appraising study of the crowd, focused his attention on her and nodded. "Sure.

Sure. This has gotta be done right." He heaved himself out of the car and came around to open the door. As he watched Cynthia alight with that too graceful, swaying carriage of hers, he grinned. "This is it, baby, so don't muff your lines. You're gonna wind up Madam Chairman."

"Madam Chairman!" Cynthia breathed it so softly Carol-Ann scarcely heard her. "Madam Chairman of the Marsten Memorial Little Theater Fund. Then they'll hafta ask me to their houses." Cynthia's chin came up. "And maybe pour tea. I been practicing, Jake. I got it down good."

"Sure, baby. Sure."

She dug her fingers into his beefy arm, released him and straightened. "You don't lift your pinky. You tuck it under."

"That's so you won't bite it by mistake," boomed Miss Emily above them. Even Jake started.

Carol-Ann looked out and up. There sat Miss Emily, looking no worse for her night's experience except, perhaps, that her iron-gray hair under that preposterous hat looked a little more like untamed steel wool than usual. She loomed above the sleek Cadillac in that great ark of a Packard, ancient enough to be a museum piece. Bailey left the wheel and went around the huge car as if it were a skittish horse. Thirty years of that infernal contraption had not convinced him it wouldn't bolt. He flung open the rear door and stepped nimbly aside, out of the way of Miss Emily's gargantuan lunge.

Jake and Cynthia, unaware of Miss Emily's usual method of descent, were not so fortunate. They were bowled over before Miss Emily braked herself to a slithering halt with her silver-knobbed stick. From his position, pinned against the Cadillac, Jake breathed heavily. "I'd like to see you do that over an open manhole."

"I like you, too. Now that the amenities are over, let's get going. I want to see which shell the pea is under."

"Huh?"

"I said I wanted to see how you thimble-rigged this party."

"Me?" Jake's look of elephantine hurt was a little overdone.

"You. To make Cynthia Chairman of the Building Fund. Everybody in town knows she's been rehearsing her speech of acceptance for a week." Miss Emily's efforts to mimic Cynthia's elegant nasal tones was not altogether a success, but the intent was there. "My deah fellow townspeople, I am overwhelmed at this most unexpected . . ."

Jake glared briefly at his wife. "Shooting off your mouth . . ."

"What do you think servants are for?" Miss Emily exonerated Cynthia. "Inside of three hours Cassie can get me more information about any family than I know about my guppies. And some of it is downright indecent." Miss Emily pivoted massively and beckoned to Carol-Ann. "Get out of that simonized sardine can and we'll go over and see Jimmy."

"Jimmy?" Cynthia scanned the crowd hastily for someone she could identify and only succeeded in locating Judge Bo bucking the crowd with timid courtesy, his Prince Albert coat and striped trousers a feeble protest against the sport shirts and slacks all around him. He made another valiant but too gentle effort to reach them, waved frantically and was engulfed. Cynthia stood on tiptoe and waved back, then smiled brightly at Miss Emily. "That was Judge Beauregard Tayloe. We bought his house, you know." Then she remembered. "Who's Jimmy?"

"Jimmy Tucker." This didn't register with Cynthia, so Miss Emily amplified. "James Bruce Tucker. The Governor.

Let's go." Miss Emily marched off. As far as Carol-Ann was concerned Miss Emily was the only person who, single-handed, could constitute a parade. However, by the time they were halfway to the pavilion they had gathered a re-spectable-sized party. Andy had slithered up from some-where, and Ronnie had bounced across the open field in his MG and left it in a single leap, to walk at Carol-Ann's other side.

They went down the standard reception line in stan-dardized style, except that near the end Ronnie leaned into Carol-Ann's ear and whispered, "Looks like an assem-bly line for turning out fraternity grips."

She had to suppress her giggle because she was face to face with Miss Thalia. "Dear Carol-Ann. So good of you. Miss Foster, may I present Governor James Bruce Tucker . . . Governor . . ." She turned to find the tall, stately man in a low-voiced conversation with Jake Scudder and hang-ing tight to Miss Emily's arm. The three made a massive rampart that Miss Thalia's frail twitterings couldn't pene-trate. But she tried, teetering around them on incredibly high heels for a woman of her age and brittle bones.

Cynthia stood by uncertainly, not knowing whether to be annoyed at not being included or honored at being so close to such distinguished company. The indecision accented her petulance.

The Governor straightened from his conversation with Jake, chuckled and thumped Jake's arm. "Good. Good. Have to remember that. First one I've heard in years I can tell on radio. Now Marsten, the old Judge, could tell some jokes that would make a mule blush, but he told 'em so well. . ."

"My father . . ." Miss Thalia, in a flare of ferocity, almost clawed her way into the group . . . "My father never let a vulgar word pass his lips! He was one of the saintliest men. He . . ." Her pale, protruding eyes glazed with righteous anger, her thin chest heaved beneath a cascade of ruffles. "He was a saint!"

"Why, Miss Marsten," the Governor looked hurt, "that is just what I've been saying. He told stories magnificently, without letting a—ah—vulgar word pass his lips. He was a—" the Governor searched for a word and handed her the perfect one—"a gentleman." And, not being one to coin a cliché lightly, he sighed, "Of the old school."

"Oh." Miss Thalia's momentary vigor seemed to have deserted her. She blinked up at him, smiling uncertainly. Almost reluctantly she returned to her social duties.

Miss Emily beamed at the Governor. "Jimmy, if you ever decide to try for ambassador, my newspapers will support you."

He twinkled at her. "It's a deal." He sighted Cynthia and stepped around the bulk of Miss Emily. "Ah, Mrs. Scudder. I was afraid you had deserted us." And very adroitly he brought her into the group. As he swung back he saw Carol-Ann still waiting. "Carol-Ann! Haven't seen you since . . ." He caught her hands and held them. "Your father's death was a great loss to the State, my dear. A great loss." He nodded gravely and then beamed around at them as if at an extraordinarily pleasant prospect. "And you'll all sit with me, won't you? It's nice to have old friends around."

The rest of the afternoon went presumably as Miss Thalia had planned it, including the *al fresco* luncheon served by the Little Theater group garbed in costumes from various of last season's successes. A subtlety that was lost on the Governor, who thought they represented epochs in history and so alluded to them in his speech.

It was an excellent speech duly extolling Virginia Beach, the great cultural contributions made by the Little Theater, and then settling down to the main text, a eulogy of Judge Theodore Clayton Marsten.

Even Carol-Ann, whose father had frequently spoken of him as "that bumbling old idiot who barely had enough sense to have the right grandfather," found herself feeling proud and humble for having known such a man. So the effect on Miss Thalia was profound. She sat up straight, her prominent eyes unfaltering on the Governor, her head nodding agreement with each new peroration. She even seemed to fill out her gaunt, dry frame and become young again. And she led the applause, happy tears streaming down her cheeks.

It was some time before Miss Emily and two other ladies had patted and soothed her back into shape to continue, but at last she stood up and signaled for the real business of the afternoon—the collecting of the Judge Theodore Clayton Marsten Memorial Little Theater Building Fund.

"You've heard what a great and public-spirited man has said of my father. More I cannot say, except that he loved the town he built and this monument we begin today will be a fitting memorial to a man who gave this town his all." It was a little incoherent and by no means accurate, but it served and was duly applauded.

"Since Mr. and Mrs. Jake Scudder have donated the grounds for the Memorial Theater," her long neck weaved to convey the idea of spacious lawns, "I think it only fitting that Mrs. Scudder be permitted to make the first contribution."

Jake nudged an unprepared Cynthia to her feet. She fumbled in her purse and drew out the check. One glance at it seemed to give her courage and she minced forward, head up. In front of the Governor—and for the Movietone camera grinding away—she paused and postured. "In behalf of this great cause, I should like to contribute one thousand dollars."

The low murmur of amazement that swept the crowd brought a triumphant smile to Cynthia's face and she gave the camera her best profile. She flourished the check at the Governor.

"You are most generous. Most generous, Mrs. Scudder. I know this will be used wisely in a worthy endeavor." He paused uncertainly, looking at the check. Then he glanced at Miss Thalia for guidance.

Thalia Marsten drew her gaunt figure to its full height, turned and surveyed the crowd, chin up, eyes alight. Slowly she swiveled and faced the Governor. "Dear James, just hand it to the Chairman of the Fund Committee."

Cynthia half extended her hand to accept the check back when Miss Thalia's next words rang across the grounds.

"The Chairman, my dear friend, Mrs. Norman Chiswell Dabney."

There wasn't a sound from the crowd. The silence stretched until it seemed an almost palpable curtain. Then it snapped with an audible twang, rising to a babble. But over it rang Cynthia's harsh voice, bitter with hate, rough with rage.

"You old bitch!"

Carol-Ann glanced around in time to see Andy duck back behind the mass of Jake Scudder, unable to mask the malicious triumph in his eyes.

6

Jake Scudder reached across Cynthia, plucked the check from the Governor's fingers and tore it in two. He stuffed the pieces deep in his pocket and caught Cynthia under the arm. "I guess we know where we stand, baby. Let's go." His voice was hoarse with the effort at control. He started forward, propelling Cynthia from the pavilion. Only his own iron control and a low-voiced "Shaddup!" prevented Cynthia from screaming fishwife vituperation at Miss Thalia. As he passed the bewildered Governor, still with his hand reaching for the check, he nodded abruptly. "Sorry, Tucker."

Carol-Ann watched them go. Cynthia stumbled in her high heels, her body wrenching and jerking against the force that propelled her. Ronnie, after a paralyzed moment, hurtled after them, his long legs loping across the field until he caught up with Jake. For an instant he trotted beside the bigger man. Then Jake turned and spoke just one word to him. Ronnie came to an abrupt halt. One hand came up slowly, massaging his jaw as if he had been struck. He passed, turned, and walked slowly to the MG.

In the agonizingly prolonged silence of the crowd Carol-Ann heard a titter behind her and turned to see Andy stifling another outburst with a fist tight against his mouth, his eyes lit with venomous amusement.

Miss Emily reached out and slapped his hand down. "Go after your sister. She needs you."

Andy glared at her, blood rising under his unhealthy pallor. He made an effort at nonchalance. "She needs me like she needs a hole in the head." He tittered nervously again. "And she's got plenty of them. I'm sticking to see the end of this hassle. I'm right interested." He grinned, his confidence returning.

Miss Emily shifted her stick ominously and he scuttled away, glaring back over his shoulder at the crowd.

"Neh-heh-heh." Miss Thalia whinnied. "That gets rid of *them.*" She straightened her thin shoulders and nodded around to the crowd in regal approval of herself and them. "Let us get on with the contributions. Governor, will you please accept the donations?"

Governor Tucker, still looking at his hand as if he expected another snatch, nodded and sat down limply. He peered from under shaggy brows at Miss Emily questioningly.

"Just sit tight, Jimmy, and take what comes." She snorted derisively. "But I did think you were enough of a politician to hang on to money once you got your hands on it."

Mrs. Dabney, looking a trifle bewildered, took her seat beside the Governor and opened a school composition book. She smiled nervously out at the crowd. "Now who's going to be first?"

There was a gentle sway of movement among the crowd but it was away from the pavilion rather than toward it. Miss Emily watched for a moment and then lumbered forward, hunched over the table and wrote out a check in front of the Governor. He leaned across the table, speaking plaintively. "Emily, get me out of this. I'm only an innocent bystander."

Miss Emily straightened, waving her check dry. She handed it to him. "Jimmy, when two women start fighting, there's no such thing as an innocent bystander." She grinned at him. "And don't worry so. When you get back to Richmond they'll give you a wound stripe. So long."

Carol-Ann made her own contribution quickly and turned away.

She caught up with Miss Emily plowing majestically through the crowd, half of which was explaining to the other half what had happened on the pavilion, with varying degrees of inaccuracy. At the outer fringes the odds seemed to favor an attempted assassination of the Governor. On one thing, however, the crowd was unanimous: whatever had happened had ended the afternoon affair. Despite the Little Theater group's valiant efforts to rally potential donors, the crowd dissolved into clickings of bumpers and bleating of horns.

At home, after a bafflingly silent ride in Miss Emily's ancient Packard, Carol-Ann started to say good-bye. She found Miss Emily staring first at the Scudders' place across the street and then Thalia Marsten's house behind her own. "I can't figure Thalia out. Just for spite she turned down one thousand dollars. For the Marsten Memorial! I don't understand it."

"Jake thought he was buying Cynthia the chairmanship with it."

"That!" Miss Emily waved it away. "So did everybody else. But nobody cared, except Thalia and a few of her fuddy-duddy friends. It's a tempest in Thalia's personal teapot. Anyway, if Thalia just wanted to hurt that Scudder female, she should have given her the job. Next to being elected tax collector, being chairman of a charity fund is about the shortest cut to unpopularity I know of." Miss Emily heaved herself up and lunged from the car. "Come in for a minute. I need a drink and somebody to listen to me cuss." She led the way up the brick walk, muttering, "Thalia was a fool to turn down that thousand dollars. But then, she's a perfect fool."

From the perspective of Miss Emily's cool side porch the afternoon looked different, less harassed. Carol-Ann could even begin to enjoy it. "Poor Cynthia . . . She thought being chairman would give her an opportunity to pour tea."

Miss Emily snorted. "That woman should first learn to pour a little oil. She's in troubled waters—" Miss Emily blinked, staring over Carol-Ann's shoulder. "Haven't seen Judge Bo in such a hurry since Old Man Carter filled his britches with buckshot—and that was fifty years ago. Bo!" she bellowed. "Beauregard!"

Judge Bo, his long, thin legs pumping in a wobbly run, his old-fashioned coattails flapping, ignored Miss Emily's imperious hail and swung across the street, headed for Jake Scudder's.

Carol-Ann gaped after him. "What on earth—"

Miss Emily settled back massively. "He's probably just learned that Jake is putting in a mullioned window where there should be a drop-sash. Nothing but that house of his could get him that excited."

Carol-Ann watched Judge Bo disappear up the walk before she turned back to Miss Emily. "But he sold it to Jake. Why should he care what Jake does with it?"

"Sold it? Jake Scudder may hold the deed to Holly Hall, and he may even live in it, Carol-Ann, but that will be Judge Bo's house till he dies. Why, his granddaddy six greats back was born there. You can't sell memories like that. Oh, Lord—" Miss Emily nudged Carol-Ann sharply. "Go stop him. Jake won't be in any mood to listen to Judge Bo's artistic complaints."

Carol-Ann was already on her way, with Miss Emily bellowing after her—"And bring him back here with you. Cassie's making plum cake with hard sauce. That ought to revive him."

Judge Bo was already at the front door as Carol-Ann rounded the japonicas. She saw that punctilious gentleman burst into a house without knocking and paused in sheer astonishment just opposite the big picture window. Jake's bellow of rage snapped her head around and she saw Ronnie standing before his uncle's big desk, his usual lopsided smile wiped away.

"So I can't, huh?" Jake's fist pounded the desk. "And who's stopping me? Not you, you sniveling little—"

"Jake!" The voice was pitched low but it carried authority. Even Jake was startled into momentary silence. A small man rose from a chair out of sight. Luke Snedicker, Jake's odd, shriveled little partner, was back. "The boy's right. You can't—"

Even from where she stood Carol-Ann could see Jake's thick neck swelling, his big fists knotting. This was certainly no time for Judge Bo to barge in. She ran for the house.

She was too late to stop him. He had already flung open the door to the den and was inside before she could reach him. At the door she halted. Cynthia stood to one side, facing the desk, her near-classic features so rigidly controlled that she seemed to wear a mask, but her fingers, digging into the fleshy upper part of her crossed arms betrayed her rage. Even the sudden intrusion did not disturb her rigidity. From the corner, sprawled in a chair, Andy watched the scene with malicious enjoyment. Judge Bo stepped forward just as Luke thrust at Jake's arm. "Sit down. Take it easy."

Jake brushed the hand away with a shrug. "Shaddup! I'm dealing with this brat." He pivoted his head slowly back to Ronnie. "Don't nobody tell Jake he can't somethin'. Now scram! Get out!"

"And stay out?" Ronnie made it so quiet that Jake had to cock his head to be sure he caught it. "That's your usual threat."

Jake's face purpled, his mouth working. Finally he exploded. "Damn it, yes! Stay out!"

Ronnie nodded. "And the next line is 'I'll cut you out of my will.' Said with fist pounding on the desk."

Jake raised his fist, looked at it and lowered it slowly. He said, with hoarse strangulation, "I've already done that. And you know it."

"Oh, I guessed." Ronnie turned to go, nodding absently to Judge Bo.

Jake bawled after him. "And you know why! I told you if you didn't give up this Betty Lou, I'd . . ."

Without looking back, Ronnie nodded. "I guessed that, too."

Jake glared at his retreating back. To have Ronnie walk out so calmly seemed to infuriate him. "Who is she? Some cheap floozy after my money. I know the type."

Ronnie stopped short. He turned back, shaking his head. "Uncle Jake, for years I've thought you were the one guy who couldn't make a mistake. It seems you can. That last crack was a mistake. It shows the chinks in the armor. Goodbye." He swung around, nodded in surprise at Carol-Ann and was gone.

Jake started around the desk after him and stumbled over his own shoes. Luke put one skinny hand on his chest, pushing him toward the chair. "Sit down, Jake. Take it easy. You can straighten things out with Ronnie later, when you've cooled off." He smiled wryly. "You always do. But right now we've got—"

Jake stared down at the thrusting hand and then up at Luke's thin, pinched face. "Take your hands off a me, worthless!"

Luke's hand whipped up, smarting Jake's cheek. "If you say that again, I'll kill you."

Judge Bo, who had stood near the door agitating in indecision, flung himself between the two men, facing Jake, a frail, elderly barrier against his rage. "Sir!"

Jake stopped in sheer amazement, glowering at the thin

fragile figure of Judge Bo. "And what the blazes do you want?"

"I want first to prevent your attacking a smaller, older man." The Judge seemed to forget, standing between the two men, that he himself was probably older and frailer than Luke. "And having done that," the Judge continued pedantically, peering up into Jake's startled face, "I shall inquire as to the truth or falsity of information that has reached me."

"Huh?" Jake stared down at the old man, his belligerence temporarily lost in incredulity. "How's that? Come again?"

Judge Bo managed to radiate dignity. "I have been informed that you have sold my home to a gambling syndicate, to be used as a gambling hall."

"Well, whadya know!" Jake reared back, glancing around the room in amusement. "The old boy's got a spy system. It ain't been an hour, and he knows about it."

"Jake!" Cynthia's voice went high. "You didn't! You gimme that house. We was gonna live there."

Jake rolled to meet this new attack. "After what happened out at the shindig? Baby, we're washed up. But this two-bit town ain't heard the last of Jake Scudder. And it ain't gonna forget him, neither. I got plans. And as for you—" He swung back to the Judge. "Sure I sold that house. It was mine, see. I bought it. At a fancy price, too, as you oughta know. So I'll sell it when I please, to who I please, for what I please." He sneered over the Judge's shoulder at Luke. "And for cash. Frank Lund pays handsome and he pays prompt. He's bringing the dough by tonight. In cash."

"Frank Lund, the gambler!" Judge Bo sighed despairingly, then drew himself up, scrawny neck thrust out over his high collar. "Then it's true."

Jake scowled down at him. "So it's true. So what?"

Judge Bo pumped himself up into new stature until he seemed nearly twice his own frail size and almost as tall as Jake. It was illusion, but the illusion of immense dignity. "Then I shall have to horsewhip you out of town."

Jake peered down in astonishment at the man and then threw back his great, bullet-shaped head and roared with laughter. "I been hit by a mouse!" One huge hand shot out and caught up the Judge's beautifully starched shirt front, and the laughter was gone. "Gonna run me outa town? You and what army?" He lifted the frail body of the Judge as if he were a puppy, held him up and marched to the door, ignoring Carol-Ann's frantic pleas to put the old man down. For answer, Jake swung the Judge around, slammed him down, put a socked foot under his coattails and shoved. The Judge spun down the hall, caroming off the walls and crashing into the glass double doors.

Carol-Ann lashed out, her small brown hand slapping Jake across the mouth. In surprise he caught her wrists, pinning them both in one huge hand. He drew back his other hand to slap her.

"Don't!" The word rang hoarsely down the hall. "Or I shall have to kill you."

Carol-Ann felt her wrists slip through Jake's fingers and saw astonishment in his eyes. He almost whispered his incredulity. "He's got a gun!"

Carol-Ann whirled and saw Judge Bo, propped feebly against the door jamb, a wicked-looking derringer in his hand. Carol-Ann ran toward him, half expecting him to collapse, but his gun hand remained steady. As she reached his side she turned.

Jake was still standing at the door of the den, staring down the hall at them. Finally, with an air that was half contempt, half bravado, he swung back into the room, leaving the door open to emphasize his contempt.

"Scram, Cyn." Jake's voice was low but penetrating. "Luke and I got things to talk about. And take that whelp with you. And you! Wipe that smirk off your face before I knock it off."

7

"Should have shot him." Miss Emily thumped her stick to emphasize the point.

Judge Bo's thin, aristocratic hand shook as he adjusted his old foulard tie. "Perhaps, if he had actually struck Carol-Ann—"

"Pooh! She could have knocked his teeth in. Ever seen her play tennis? Or drive a golf ball?"

Judge Bo twisted in his chair. "He sold *my* house to that—gambler. The idea! The home of the Tayloes—a gambling hall!"

"Pish! No need to worry about your house. Lund can't touch it."

"He can't?" Judge Bo looked momentarily cheerful and then sighed. "But Scudder sold it to him. He's paying for it tonight. In cash."

"We'll get an injunction. Commercial use in a residential area."

Judge Bo started to relax, then shook his head. "But it isn't in a residential area. It's out in the county. He could—"

"Publicity. Plenty of publicity. Gamblers and crooks can't stand it. Gamblers especially. Starts the Internal Revenue people looking at tax returns. I didn't watch the Kefauver Committee for nothing. No, I wouldn't worry about your house. It may not be strictly legal, but get an injunction. Any grounds will do. And we'll scream about it in my newspapers. Nothing makes me feel so righteous as knowing I'm wrong in a right cause."

Carol-Ann found herself relaxing, considering the frail, elderly judge in his outmoded manners and clothes, wondering at the brief flare of wrath he couldn't sustain. He lived in the past, and not even his own past, but one long dead and gone.

But why had Jake so suddenly sold the house? Because Miss Thalia had slammed a door in Cynthia's face? There was more to it than that, Carol-Ann felt sure. Jake had said violently that he had plans.

Cassie rumped the swinging door aside and pivoted majestically in, planting her splayed feet directly in front of Carol-Ann. "Take that dish on the corner," she ordered. "It got an extra dollop of hard sauce. Do you good after what that blackhearted scoundrel done." Food was Cassie's solution to almost any crisis. She pivoted heavily to Judge Bo. "That there one is yours, Judge. Got a mite more brandy on it."

Cassie turned to eye Miss Emily. "I wasn't figuring on servin' you none, but I reckon I'll give it to you now. Druther do that than have you traipsing around for it after midnight and getting bopped on the head."

Judge Bo clucked. "I heard about your dreadful experience. Terrible. Terrible. Don't know what the Beach is coming to. It's this lawless Yankee element getting in. I think we should form a posse and—"

"Don can handle it," Carol-Ann contributed.

"Don?" Judge Bo glanced at Miss Emily for help.

Miss Emily dripped melting hard sauce, caught it expertly with her tongue and sighed happily. "A policeman."

"Oh!" As if that accounted for his not knowing him.

"I'm going to marry him." Carol-Ann licked the underside of the spoon.

"Oh!" He turned hurriedly to Miss Emily, as if this were something best passed over. "I hope you weren't seriously hurt."

"Nope." Miss Emily was laconic when eating.

"It must have been a dreadful experience, just the same. The curlers probably saved you from serious injury." He laughed faintly. "At least those hideous things have some useful purpose."

"Useful?" Miss Emily even laid aside her spoon to pursue this topic. "Without curlers a woman would be a social loss. Without curlers, she would be a lank-haired drudge. Why, without curlers, many a woman would never get married. I caught my Fred with curlers." Miss Emily picked up her spoon and held it triumphantly, like a sceptre.

"I never married." Judge Bo said it quietly, bending over his plate.

Miss Emily, digging into her plum cake, paused thoughtfully and murmured, "Thalia."

Judge Bo nodded. "But it was not to be. Judge Marsten did not approve, and Thalia wouldn't think of going against his wishes. She adored him." He sighed gently. "I suppose he felt I wasn't the man for her."

Miss Emily's spoon clattered angrily. "Nonsense. He was a pompous old stuffed shirt—and selfish as the devil. Thalia waited on him hand and foot—and he wasn't giving up a good thing. He chased off every man that hung around Thalia. And she let him. No spunk. No spine. No git-up-and-git."

"She was so delicate, so fragile. . . ."

"Poppycock!" Miss Emily shook her spoon at him. "Also eyewash. You know as well as I do that Thalia could ride and swim and sail a boat as well as any man. All the Marstens could. But the Judge developed an allergy to horses. So Thalia gave up her four-gaited hunter. The Judge liked sailing until he got rich enough to go to Europe and got seasick. And if the Judge didn't like sailing, Thalia gave up boats. I've always thought that was one reason Ted holds on to his lugger. It was his one escape from the Judge's petty tyranny—and now, from Thalia, when she gets too possessive."

"That's most unkind, Emily!" Miss Thalia stood in the kitchen doorway looking limp and tragic. "I didn't mean to eavesdrop. I just came to . . . to . . ." Tears welled in her prominent eyes and she blinked them away. "I didn't expect you to be cruel—and him just dead."

Miss Emily reared back in astonishment. "Don't be so darn dramatic, Thalia. The Judge has been dead nearly thirty years."

"Not Father—Ted." Miss Thalia wailed thinly, clamping a gaunt fist against her withered lips. "Gone."

"Ted? But he—I just got a card." Miss Emily gestured vaguely toward her desk; then realization hit. She lumbered to her feet, levering herself on her stick.

Judge Bo reached Thalia first. With an arm around her thin, quivering shoulders, he led her to a chair. Carol-Ann ran to the bathroom for ammonia. When she returned Thalia was seated, her gaunt hands convulsively clasping one of Judge Bo's, and Miss Emily was bellowing for Cassie and hot soup.

Miss Emily scowled darkly. "I'm truly sorry, Thalia, to hear about Ted. When did it happen?"

Miss Thalia ate a spoonful of soup and shook her head. "I don't know." And then, realizing this needed some explanation, she fumbled in her pocket and produced a crumpled telegram. "I got this." She held it out to Judge Bo.

He read it, and passed it on to Miss Emily, who read it aloud. "We regret to inform you of the death of your brother, Theodore Marsten, aboard his boat. Details follow. Signed, Captain Osiah Melton, U.S. Coast Guard, Albemarle Sound Station."

Miss Emily laid the paper in her lap, smoothing it with her hands. "I'm truly sorry. I was fond of Ted." Suddenly, as if something had occurred to her, she grabbed up the telegram again, studying it. She lowered it, glancing perplexedly at Miss Thalia. "This was sent yesterday."

Miss Thalia started another spoonful of soup toward her mouth. She nodded, then gulped.

"You've known it since yesterday—and didn't tell anybody?" Miss Emily was incredulous.

"Oh. Emily!" Thalia laid down her spoon deliberately. "I couldn't. Why, if people had known, they might have expected me to call off the Memorial Party to dear Father. And I just couldn't. I really couldn't. It meant so much!" Her old, withered face crumpled like wet tissue paper and she dropped her head in her hands, sobbing. "And it turned out so awful. Just awful. Almost nobody gave anything. And all on account of that horrible woman. And that horrid man, vulgarly snatching back that check from the hand of the Governor. The Governor! A thousand dollars! You heard her say it. A thousand dollars! Why, that would have bought—"

"Thalia!" Miss Emily thumped peremptorily with her stick. "Get hold of yourself. I know you're overwrought. Ted's death had been a shock, but you must keep your perspective. You started that. You let Jake Scudder think that Cynthia would be chairman if he gave the grounds and a thousand dollars. You sold him something. And didn't deliver."

Miss Thalia set the soup plate carefully aside and stood up. "And what if I did? If he'd been a gentleman he—"

"If he'd been a gentleman, there wouldn't have been any deal to make."

"He shouldn't have grabbed that check back."

"I think that was the smartest thing he's done since he hit Virginia Beach."

"And I thought you were my friend." Miss Thalia threw back her head on its scrawny neck and stalked to the door. "Bo, you may escort me home."

"Yes, Thalia." Judge Bo cut his eyes around at Miss Emily and breathed deeply, pinching in his nostrils. "Emily, I really had expected more of you than this." He started after Miss Thalia, who had disappeared.

Miss Emily watched him go and turned back to Carol-Ann with a rueful sigh. "And after I'd fixed him up with his first date in over forty years."

Carol-Ann touched her arm lightly. "Later on they'll understand."

"Not those two. They're living on lavender and old lace." Miss Emily levered herself up and started for the phone. "I'd better get somebody to go stay with Thalia tonight. Who's sympathetic and dim-witted?"

"I'll stay with her." Carol-Ann giggled. "Not that I think I'm dim-witted, or even especially sympathetic, but I can be firm and even bossy, and order sleeping powders and hot water bottles and ice packs and lots of rest. That ought to do the trick. Anyway, I don't want to go back to that house tonight." She indicated her own house with a brief nod. "Everybody is too wrought up."

Taking over was surprisingly less trouble than she had anticipated, except for Miss Thalia's brief outburst of tears as they listened to a meager radio report on the finding of Ted's body aboard his boat in Albemarle Sound. Death was attributed to a sailing accident.

"He was so young, so strong, so brave," Miss Thalia pronounced through a mist of tears, turning off the radio. Her grief, however, shifted to long moments of bemused silence broken with little half-giggles that Carol-Ann attributed to the memory of Judge Bo's visit. Briefly the idea occurred to Carol-Ann that some good might come of Ted's death. If it brought Judge Bo and Miss Thalia together they might find a few years of happiness.

She was dreamily co-operative about undressing and going to bed and agreed that a hot water bottle was just the thing and one small sleeping pill was all she needed. She smiled plaintively at Carol-Ann from the unbecoming frou-frou of a ruffled pink bed jacket. "Just leave me alone with my thoughts. Thoughts and prayers." She smiled again, shyly. "And hopes."

Carol-Ann left her and went down the gloomy hall to the room Miss Thalia had offered her—rather tactlessly—for its obvious heavy masculinity had only recently been Ted's.

She pulled a chair around and hung her blue and gold kimono handily across the back, slid out of her mules and slid gratefully between the sheets, dropping off almost at once into healthy sleep.

It seemed almost immediately that she leapt from the bed into the dark terrors of an unfamiliar room, yet she was surer hours had passed than she was of what had awakened her. She slid her feet into the waiting mules and groped uncertainly for the robe. She wriggled into it and stood up, still wondering what had awakened her. Then she heard it again.

Miss Thalia screamed.

8

"That's the loudest case of hysterics I ever heard," Miss Emily announced from the kitchen door. She thumped her way into the dining room, momentarily blocking Carol-Ann's view. "And what were you planning to do with that cook book? Boil the burglar?"

Miss Thalia stopped in mid-scream, quivered gulpily and peered at the cook book. Very daintily she held it far out from her and let go.

"And get down off the sideboard." Miss Emily squinted at Miss Thalia crouched among the Marsten silver, her angular arms and bony knees huddled into a tight, quivering knot. "How the devil did you get up there?" Honest bafflement rode in Miss Emily's voice.

"I jumped."

Miss Emily goggled. "Jumped?"

"I jumped." Miss Thalia attempted dignity atop the sideboard. "I turned on the lights and saw those footprints and jumped."

Miss Emily measured the distance from the light switch to the sideboard and sighed. "You should be in the Olympics. Now get down, Thalia."

Miss Emily glanced at the low window seat, went over to verify their reality with her fingertip. Muddy footprints. One large, moist, loamy footprint in the middle

63

of the flowered cretonne cushion. Left foot. Right foot on Miss Thalia's waxed hardwood floor in damp outline. Left foot again on the creamy inner border of the hooked rug. Miss Emily stared at this for a long moment and then peered up at the leaded green glass monstrosity of a light fixture as if she expected to find the burglar up there.

A low chuckle at the archway swung her around to face Don Corley, who glanced derisively up at the Edwardian horror that had been Judge Marsten's pride and joy. "He's not up there."

Miss Emily's stick pointed out the three footprints one by one, from the window seat and heading toward the archway. "Burglars flee, not fly."

Don entered the room lightly, almost on tiptoe, as if he were afraid of disturbing the footprints. Then he, too, peered up at the inverted green glass dome.

"He's not up there," Miss Emily mimicked, folding her hands over the knob of her stick and leaning on it.

"Yeah." As if he realized this wasn't brilliant dialogue, he thrust his flat-brimmed hat to the back of his head and glared at the footprint.

Carol-Ann, deciding Miss Thalia was reasonably secure on her perch, went over to stand by Don, just so he'd be handy in case she might decide to faint after all.

Don caught her shoulders, half turning her. For a delirious instant she thought he was going to kiss her right there. Instead he aimed her at the kitchen, starting her off with a light shove.

"If you're going to be sick, don't mess up the footprint. It's evidence."

Miss Emily chuckled. "She's trying being helpless."

"Oh, no!" Don lifted his eyes piously. "Dear Lord, not that! She's about as helpless as a Sherman tank."

"I saw a man," Miss Thalia had been neglected long enough, "a huge man, in the window."

Don walked over to stand beside the scrawny figure perched on the sideboard. "Was he going out or coming in?"

Miss Thalia's long, pointed tongue whipped out, licking at her thin lips and folded back in. Her prominent eyes bugged with the effort to concentrate. At last she shook her head. "I don't know. But when I turned on the lights he was gone." Her smile pleaded with Don for understanding. "So he must have been going out, mustn't he?"

"Did you recognize him?"

Miss Thalia shut her eyes and waved her hands in slow, mystic motions. "I see . . . I see . . ." Slowly she dropped her arms and sighed. "No. There's nothing." She opened her eyes suddenly and thrust her face close to Don's. "But those footprints. You can send them to the FBI in Washington and they—"

"That's fingerprints."

Don sighed and turned back to the three baffling footprints. He even stepped on the window seat, over Miss Thalia's squeal of protest, and, carefully avoiding the original, set his left foot down. He took a step, his right alongside the second footprint and then again on his left, standing with his right foot in the air, wobbling uncertainly. For a good four feet in any direction there was a creamy expanse of hooked rug, unmarked by prints. He appealed to Miss Emily. "What did he do then?"

"Helicopter," suggested Miss Emily. "And put your other foot down. You make me dizzy, swaying like that."

Don set his foot down, carefully straddling the print. "Helicopter!"

Miss Emily shrugged massively. "He took off his shoes," she offered Don.

"In the dark? While standing on one foot?" Don tugged at his ear and groaned. "I wouldn't want to try it, but I suppose I'll have to buy that." He glared down once more at the footprint. "Because we know it must have happened. I'd sure give a pretty penny to know how."

"He sat down and took them off—"

"Why, I think that's very clever," Miss Thalia approved from her grandstand seat. "Are you psychic, Emily?"

"With one foot in the air?" Don demonstrated again, attempting to sit down with one foot off the floor. He wobbled so erratically that Miss Emily had to steady him. "And why?" Don pointed to the print. "He'd already left three prints. Which he didn't bother to rub out. So why take off his shoes at this point?"

Carol-Ann turned from her inspection of the window seat and the tall, narrow window behind it. "I still can't figure out how he got through such a narrow window. He's awfully big." Carol-Ann ballooned out her cheeks and molded a paunch in the air. "Hefty."

Don strode over to her. "So you know he's big—and hefty."

"Well," Carol-Ann knew she was aggravating him, and it pleased some perverse feminine element in her she hadn't suspected was there. She made her eyes wide and soulful. "Well, Miss Thalia said—"

Don blinked away from her eyes. "Don't do that. You remind me of a sick calf. Miss Foster, the time for games has passed. Will you answer a few simple questions?"

"Yes." Carol-Ann made it very meek because, now that she knew, the whole thing seemed a little ridiculous. Miss Thalia had never been in any danger. It was all a rather impractical practical joke.

"How can you be sure his shoes didn't squeak?"

"Because they don't. They never do. He wears very fine shoes."

Don took a deep breath, then let it out slowly, his hands clenching. "You mean you know whose shoes made those prints?"

"Of course."

"Then why the . . ." He caught himself up. "Why didn't you tell us before this?"

"I didn't get to see them. You shooed me away."

"Oh." Don wilted. He stood silent a moment; then, taking another long breath, he asked her formally, "Miss Foster, now that you have had an opportunity to examine the footprints, will you tell us who made them?"

"Well," Carol-Ann pretended to study the print again, but its pattern was already familiar enough, "they're from Jake Scudder's shoes, and he usually wears 'em but not often."

Don turned dazedly away from Carol-Ann and stared down at the print on the window seat.

"Jake Scudder?"

Miss Thalia screamed once more and fainted among the Marsten silver service.

9

"I don't believe it!" It wasn't that Don really questioned her statement. He simply seemed incapable of believing that Jake Scudder had made those prints. "Why would a man like Scudder come sneaking in here at night?"

"Well . . ." Miss Thalia, revived by three slaps from Miss Emily and a little flushed from a glass of sherry, bridled coyly. "He thought I was here alone—a woman." She clasped her emaciated arms across the flatness of her bosom and shivered. A faint flush mottled her gaunt cheeks.

Carol-Ann suppressed a giggle. She looked up to see Don eyeing her sternly.

"Miss Foster, would you be willing to face Jake Scudder with the statement you just made?"

She suppressed another giggle and nodded. "They're his, all right. I'd recognize them anywhere. He has his shoes specially made. In London. With that odd, squiggly ground-gripper sole." Carol-Ann drew zig-zags in the air with her finger.

"You're probably right. Anyway, we can soon check." He glared again at the three footprints that stopped in the middle of the cream-colored rug. "And maybe he'll tell us how he did it." He grinned. "Right now that baffles me more than the 'why' of it."

"Oh!" Miss Thalia almost whistled the word in her excitement. "The deed."

Don whirled on her. "What deed?"

Miss Thalia shrank back in her chair, looking pitiful.

"What deed would Jake want?"

Miss Emily leaned forward on her stick. "She's talking about the deed Scudder gave her to the grounds where they're going to put up the Marsten Memorial Little Theater."

Don nodded.

"It's to be a memorial to dear Father. That man gave me the deed. I don't keep it in the house, naturally, but he wouldn't know that."

"He'd know enough to know stealing the deed wouldn't do him any good. The transfer has already been recorded when the deed is issued, most likely."

"You mean—stealing a deed wouldn't do any good? Oh, dear, oh dear." Miss Thalia sighed profoundly. "And I was so sure . . ."

"While they're photographing these prints we might as well go over and talk to Scudder." He nodded to Carol-Ann.

"At three in the morning?" Carol-Ann protested. "They'll all be asleep."

Don pointed to the footprints. "Somebody wasn't asleep twenty minutes ago."

"Let's go." Miss Emily levered herself up.

"No need for you to go, Miss Emily."

She aimed her stick at the final print on the rug. "You don't think I could sleep tonight till I find out how he did that, do you?"

Light gleamed softly behind the drawn drapes of the picture window. "Someone's still up," Don pointed out, and led Carol-Ann to the porch, banging on the old brass knocker. Lights sprang up, fanned out through the side-lights of the door. A bolt and chain rattled. Behind her Carol-Ann heard a gasp, and then Miss Thalia's voice, quivery and indignant, "Why, she locked the door! Nobody at Virginia Beach ever locks doors." The door was flung open.

Cynthia stood in the doorway, outlined in light. A little too well outlined, in Carol-Ann's opinion. "Ye-uss?" Cynthia was being her most ladylike. Carol-Ann nudged Don into speech.

"We'd like to speak to Ja . . . to Mister Scudder."

Cynthia sniffed delicately. "Mister Scudder does not receive at this . . ." She leaned forward, peering into the dark as if she had noticed Carol-Ann for the first time. "Well, really, my dear. . ." Her voice was extremely refined. "I didn't expect to see you here again. Not ahhfter that disgraceful scene this ahfternoon."

"Wipe your chin, Cynthia. Your culture's dripping." Carol-Ann thoroughly enjoyed the stricken look on Cynthia's face before she covered it again with the shaky mask of extreme gentility. "Don't bother to make like a lady. This lug doesn't like 'em. Anyway, he's only a policeman."

Cynthia dragged venomous eyes from Carol-Ann and smiled out at Don. "A policeman! Oh, dear, I just know there's been another of those silly, silly robberies. I thought I heard sirens. That must have been what waked me. But really, we cahn't help you. And it is quite late." She smiled. "Perhaps some other time." She made a half-hearted effort to shut the door, but Don stepped in.

"I'm afraid I'll have to speak to Mister Scudder." He paused as Cynthia failed to back up. It put them extremely close. Carol-Ann got a nice feminine enjoyment out of Don's blush. "Now." He made it firm.

"I—" Cynthia backed off, wriggling peevishly. "I—" She glanced down the hall to the closed doors of the den. "I wouldn't want to disturb him. He's been in conference with his partner for hours—simply hours."

"Nonsense!" Luke Snedicker's thin, dry voice preceded his thin dry figure around the turn in the hall by a fraction of a second. "You know perfectly well, Cynthia, that I've been in bed—at least in my room—since midnight. Hullo?" He leaned forward to peer beyond Cynthia. "Who's there? Oh, a policeman. Andy's in trouble again, I suppose. What is it this time? Speeding? Or drunken driving?" He strutted down the hall as he talked, tightening the belt of his bathrobe with quick, nervous fingers. As he came to Cynthia he peered up at her. "And what made you say I was still talking to Jake?"

Cynthia backed off, her lower lip protruding sullenly. "Well, somebody's been in there with him. For hours." Culture was wearing thin, rubbed away by anger. "Ev'y time I wanna say som'pin to him, there's somebody there. And Ronnie's gone and Andy's out."

"You might invite these people in, Cynthia. I assume," Luke gestured politely, "they did want to come in."

Cynthia aroused from her petulance long enough to revive her gentility. "Won't you come in, Mister—er—"

"Corley. Sergeant Don Corley."

"Mister Corley. And Miss Carol-Ann."

Carol-Ann gritted her teeth. That woman was doing it again. Miss Carol-Ann! As if Carol-Ann were a generation older. Carol-Ann stepped past her and spoke to Luke, who seemed mildly surprised to see her step out of the dark. He almost lost his nervous grip on his belt as Miss Emily loomed through the door.

"Welcome to our domicile, Miss Emily, and . . . and . . ." Cynthia almost boggled at Miss Thalia, who swept in belligerently in Miss Emily's broad wake. Cynthia turned back to the door for another greeting. The sight of Cassie, armed and belligerent, swamped her. There was no rule in Cynthia's book for greeting servants.

Miss Emily solved her dilemma by calling over her massive shoulder. "You stick with me, Cassie."

Miss Emily, with unerring instinct, located the most comfortable chair, even in that gloom, and plopped herself down, while Cassie took up uneasy guardianship just behind her. Miss Thalia twittered uncertainly between two nearly identical chairs. Finally she settled on the edge of one. Carol-Ann picked one end of a hideous rose-back sofa.

Luke came in behind them, leaving Cynthia and Don in the hall. He ducked his head slightly and peered around as if he, too, had difficulty with Cynthia's manufactured gloom. He seemed to be cataloguing them with a trader's shrewd eye to future purchase or sale. He picked Carol-Ann as a known starter and smiled vaguely at her. "Mrs. Tilworthy." He had pinned Miss Emily down. He skipped Cassie's armed truculence and peered at Miss Thalia. "Miss Marstens?" It was tentative. A feeler.

"Yes?" Miss Thalia chirruped, tilting her head.

"I—er—we were quite distressed to hear of your brother's death. I never had the pleasure of knowing him, but Jake has spoken of him so often. They seemed quite close."

Miss Thalia lifted her small, receding chin until it almost seemed to jut. "That is most unlikely. My brother was most particular." She delivered that with a finality that closed the conversation at a blank dead end.

Luke coughed softly behind his hand and peered around for an unoccupied chair. He was still half stooping when Cynthia swept in, almost unseating the little man.

She flurried in, swishing her peignoir, her breath almost whistling through pinched nostrils. "You!" She seemed to locate Carol-Ann more by instinct than sight.

She bore down on her, arms hugged under her heaving bosom. She stood over Carol-Ann, twisting, shaking herself into rage. Then her voice skirled off into high brass, her stinging twang describing Carol-Ann in terms that she found amazingly lucid though she had never, to the best of her knowledge, heard any of them. Carol-Ann found herself appraising them with almost critical detachment, marveling at the fluidity and clarity of profanity. Then their application sunk in. She stood up and swung. Her hand smacked Cynthia's head sideways. The torrent died to a whimper.

Cynthia put a hand slowly to her face.

"Surprised? I didn't know all the words, but I guessed. They seemed to call for that. Ladies sometimes pack a mean wallop, Cynthia, so look out."

Don came pounding in, trying to get between them, but Carol-Ann glared him away. Somewhere off in the gloom Miss Emily chortled. She dearly loved a good fight. Luke came up from behind and caught Cynthia's rocking elbows.

"What the devil is this, Cynthia?"

"Her. The little—" Luke shook her violently and she stopped, whimpered, began again. "She's been playing around with Jake. Little Miss Innocence!"

Carol-Ann stared through narrowed eyes at Cynthia's raddled, convulsed face. "If Jake even so much as made a pass at me, I'd give him just what you got—or a knife in the ribs, if it was handy."

"Did you?"

The words hung in the air like reverberations from a cheap brass gong. Carol-Ann sensed their ominousness.

"Did I what?"

"Stick a knife in him?" Cynthia shrilled. "That's how he died."

She whirled and collapsed against Don, sobbing.

10

"Emily, dear, your best bone-handled knife!" Miss Thalia, with that characteristic of some very frail people, was standing up remarkably well in the face of actual trage-dy. She stared down at Jake Scudder sprawled in his big leather chair, his head thrown back in a ghastly parody of laughter.

"He wasn't expecting it." Miss Emily braced herself on her stick and peered down at Jake. "But then, none of us ever is. What I mean is, I don't think he even realized he was being killed. He looks almost as if he was enjoying a huge joke."

Don, looking a little disheveled after a session with Cynthia's hysterics, nodded solemn agreement. "Could be." He surveyed the undisturbed surface of the desk, the few papers scattered to one side on the floor. "Not much blood. But with a single, swift stab like that, there never is. The killer must have taken him by surprise."

Miss Emily pivoted to peer at the big double doors fac-ing the desk and then at the outside door to the right that led to the garden and garage. "You couldn't sneak in and surprise him. So it had to be someone he knew. And knew pretty intimately."

Don started to shake his head, thought better of it and nodded. "His checkbook."

Miss Emily glanced at him in pleased surprise. "It's open. I never saw a business man yet who didn't shut his checkbook when somebody stood close to his desk. Unless he's going to pay 'em something. And Jake," she tapped the checks fanned loosely across the desk, "was checking his balance."

"A man might open his checkbook to prove something." Don said it tentatively, his eyes on a corner of the room. Miss Emily encouraged him with a nod. "Like he can't pay until Monday—or else he's got enough to cover the check he's giving. Was he giving somebody a check?"

Don studied the checkbook. "No. The last three are for milk, the laundry and lights." He indicated three sealed envelopes. "And he was mailing those." He looked directly at Miss Emily.

"Somebody he knew pretty well stood by his desk, saw the knife . . ." She swung around on Carol-Ann. "You did say the knife was here this afternoon?"

Carol-Ann shut her eyes for a moment, seeing Jake slamming his fist down, nicking his thumb.

"Yes, it was here."

"The killer picked up the knife. Jake is leaning forward, maybe pointing out something. The killer sticks the knife at his back. Jake feels the first prick and rears back. The knife jams against the leather of the chair—and goes in."

"You make it sound almost accidental." Don stooped to peer between the chair and body.

"Not accidental. Anyone who took a knife to Jake would have to go all the way—or regret it. No, I was just trying to figure out how he got in that position." Miss Emily sighed wearily. "And now I'll never know how he made those footprints." She moved around the desk and finally levered herself until she could peer around Jake's legs into the kneehole. She harumphed loudly twice and thrust herself back up, glaring at Don.

"He didn't."

"Huh?"

"He didn't make those footprints. He's in his sock feet." Miss Emily's eyes prowled the room angrily while Don stooped to confirm her statement. "And his shoes aren't anywhere in here. And anyway, if it was him, how'd he make only three prints and no more?"

"We're back to them?" Don asked it wearily.

"Yes. And I like it this way. After the murder, the killer saw the shoes by the desk. Carol-Ann told me he slips 'em off as soon as he comes in. The killer slipped into Jake's shoes—almost anybody could have gotten both a foot and shoe into one of those gunboats of his—and left."

"Why? I mean, why leave in Jake's shoes?"

"He had to go out through the garden door. Remember, that Scudder female had to unbolt the front door for us, so he didn't go out that way. But out that door is the garden, where he'd leave footprints."

"If it's a he—and if he ever left the house." Don, apparently, was developing his own ideas.

"*Somebody* left here. In Jake's shoes. And went over to Thalia's, climbed in the window, made those three prints and simply stepped out of the shoes. They were big enough. He could have done it without even bending over. Then his own shoes didn't leave any prints because they didn't get garden loam on them."

Yes, a person with much smaller feet could have slipped into Jake's shoes and made the three prints. But it would have had to be a small person, and Miss Thalia had shrilled excitedly of a huge man. Then Carol-Ann remembered. Once, in the dark, Don had looked immense and menacing. To Miss Thalia, any figure against her window would

have looked big. And Jake could so easily have let in the
killer at the front door, locked and bolted it. After the
murder, he'd slip out through the garden—and Jake's shoes
would be ideal to mask footprints. Carol-Ann could visu-
alize it all perfectly—except for a face. And a reason. Miss
Emily had answered one question and left a dozen wide
open.

Don seemed to feel it, too. He banged lightly at the
side of his nose, his lips tight, his eyes hot and angry.
"That's about all we can do here 'till the Coroner comes,
and the lab boys test the place." He started herding them
out of the office.

"We're locking up this room, Snedicker, until the Coroner and the lab boys get here."

Snedicker nodded. "I finally got Mrs. Scudder calmed
down. She's in the living room." He scanned the den hurriedly, took a second look at Jake and started to back out.
"What did you do with the money? Put it in the safe?"

"Money?" Don quirked his head around. "I didn't see
any money." He started for the desk. "Unless it's under
these papers."

Snedicker shook his head. "Sixty thousand dollars is
too big a bulk for—"

"Sixty thousand dollars!" Don came to a dead halt, pivoted slowly. "Sixty thousand dollars? Did Jake keep that
much money on hand? In cash?"

"Not usually. But Frank Lund paid him . . ."

"Lund? The gambler?"

"I've heard him called a gambler." Snedicker's high,
thin voice was precise. "But that statement would have
to—"

"That Scudder person." Miss Thalia pointed an arthrit-
ic finger at the dead man. "Him. He did sell Bo's lovely
old home to that ruffian." She gasped anew. "Oh, this will
kill poor dear Beauregard— Dear Bo!"

"It seems to have killed Jake," Snedicker pointed out dryly, then turned hastily to Don. "Not that I mean to imply that that is the motive. But if sixty thousand is missing, it could very easily be the reason."

"True. But the money could be in the safe, or a desk drawer, or the filing cabinet." As Snedicker started forward Don put out a hand, thrusting the little man back. "And it'll have to wait till the lab boys get through in here. I'm locking up."

Carol-Ann let herself be herded into the hall along with the others, almost unable to realize that Jake, who had been so vital, was really dead.

Miss Emily's arm went around her shoulders, oddly comforting, but her words sent another shudder down Carol-Ann's spine. "I'm leery of a man who's too polite. I wonder what Snedicker's covering up? Murder?"

Luke Snedicker lingered at the door, listening to Don lock up after them. He caught Carol-Ann listening, too, and whisked a smile at her. "We'll all be much happier when we know the money is gone."

"If it was ever there," Miss Emily answered.

Luke stopped in midstride. "It was there. Frank said he'd pay tonight. He paid. A gambler's word has to be good."

"Oh, you admit he's a gambler."

Luke smiled coldly. "To you, yes. To the police, no. I handle a lot of financing on government contracts. I can't afford to know gamblers." He sighed. "Neither could Jake, it seems."

Don slid in the front door, threw Carol-Ann a brief smile and led the way into the living room.

Cynthia, now composed, had taken command of a low, ultra-modern chair that suited her but not the room. She leaned well back, so that the barrel-shade lighted half her face dramatically and spotlighted her figure. Watching

Cynthia, Carol-Ann missed the first of Don's questioning and heard only Cynthia's answer.

" . . . I was in my boudoir, sound asleep, when I heard you pounding on the door, so I'm afraid I cahn't help you. Jake had visitors, yes. I heard 'em earlier. Luke was with him, too, for simply hours."

"I left him at midnight, Cynthia. You know it. I spoke to you when I caught you in the hall."

"Caught me?" Cynthia tinkled gayly at this absurdity. "Luke, dear, you make it sound as if I were sneaking around my own house."

"Weren't you?" Snedicker tightened his mouth into a prim smile. "I got the distinct impression you were—listening."

"Why, you—" Cynthia glared, then huddled back in the chair, sulking. "I shoulda slapped that smirk offa your puss then."

Snedicker nodded. "At least we've established I was in the hall—leaving the den."

Cynthia ducked to peer around the barrel shade at Don. "You gonna let this slug— Hey!" Her eyes fastened on Carol-Ann, ran up and down her like malicious mice. "That kimono! I saw you in it. Tonight."

Carol-Ann caught the blue-and-gold robe tighter. "You could have. Easily. I threw it around my shoulders when I took my things over to Miss Thalia's. It was simpler that way, with both hands full." She knew she was saying too much. It sounded false, but she was trying to reconstruct for herself when Cynthia could have seen it. She'd only worn it once before, to run over to Miss Emily's because the old flannel one she loved was getting too shabby for visiting. "Or you might have seen it last night. Yes, I'm sure you did, because that's when I brought the—" For the first time the ghastly truth hit her. She had brought the knife into this house—and it had killed Jake.

"It has a gold dragon on the back," Cynthia said furiously, as if that proved something. "And I saw it when you left here. Under the street light."

"That was about eleven, when I went to stay with Miss Thalia."

"I know when I seen it!" Cynthia swooped out of the chair to face Carol-Ann. "Not an hour ago, when you sneaked outa Jake's den—"

"But, Mrs. Scudder, that's impossible." Miss Thalia almost whinnied her "impossible." "Simply impossible. The dear child was asleep when I went downstairs and found those horrid prints. I peeked in on her—" Miss Thalia's thin brows rose as she peered around an imaginary door. "And I heard her breathing."

"She can breathe like a porpoise for all I care! All I know is, I seen her in the dragon robe, sneaking outa this house at two-thirty."

"Did you?" Miss Emily's voice was almost purringly sweet, which should have warned Cynthia.

"You're darn right I did. Right through that window—" Cynthia pointed with dramatic fervor to the other picture window that marred the living room.

"Now isn't that odd—and just a little difficult, don't you think?"

"What's odd about it?" Cynthia swept to the window and pushed aside the drapes. "I can see the whole front yard and the street right under the light and . . ." She faltered, turning back into the room, her eyes on Miss Emily bright and hot with rage.

Miss Emily smiled at her. "So you've realized it might have been difficult, especially since you were up in your boudoir, sound asleep."

11

"Since your boudoir is upstairs at the back of the house," Miss Emily pointed out with surprising calm, "I would say, Mrs. Scudder, that it's a question of which story you care to be stuck with."

"I—" Cynthia's mouthing came to an abrupt halt, her eyes narrowed. "I guess it was eleven o'clock when I saw her. Really, I'm so upset, I'm a little confused." She rubbed her hand across her forehead, carefully watching her curls. "Yes, it was eleven o'clock. It must have been."

Something was troubling Carol-Ann—a vague, nagging memory of something very slight, meaningless at the time but now with a glimmering of importance. What was it? Oh, yes. . . . She had cold chills, because she knew now why someone had worn Jake's outsized shoes all the way to Miss Thalia's. She smiled at Cynthia.

"You know, Cynthia, I don't see how you keep your hair so lovely."

Surprised, Cynthia touched her forehead, ran her fingers softly up the elaborate hair-do, a self-satisfied smile beginning. Suddenly the hand quivered; the smile disappeared. "You stinking, lousy little—" Cynthia started for Carol-Ann but Don caught her, swung her around, shaking her.

"What the— All she said was—" Don thrust himself at arm's length from Cynthia's writhing and stared at the intricate pile of tortured curls. "Oh! The hair-do!" He appealed to Carol-Ann. "That what you mean?" He released one hand long enough to pantomime the swirls and convolutions of Cynthia's hair. "Don't women usually . . . I mean, when they go to bed—" He flushed. "I mean . . ."

In his astonishment Don released Cynthia momentarily and then made another grab for her as she started toward Carol-Ann.

Cynthia's tactics, however, had changed. She almost slithered forward, her mouth twisting. "All right, Miss Smarty Pants! So my hair's on straight. So I didn't go to bed. So I was up." She laughed shrilly. "And you've put me on the spot." She laughed again. "But don't forget, baby, that puts you right back on the spot with me. 'Cause I *was* up—and I *did* see you. And it was two-thirty, not eleven!"

She whirled on Don. "Yeah, I was up. In this room. And I seen her in that dragon kimono, sneaking across the street. She'd been in there with Jake." Cynthia broke then, her voice dropping from its shrill, brassy skirl to a throaty catch. "She was with him. I heard him laugh. . . .

"Maybe he wasn't no gentleman, but he was my man." It died to a whisper. "And he's gone." Her control slipped, and the classic face crumpled.

Carol-Ann started up to go to her in sympathy but Cynthia glared sullenly at her.

"Stay put, kid." She faced Don, and even in the half-light she looked haggard. "So I lied a little. But I'm telling you straight, copper. I heard Jake laughing. I'd been waiting up for him 'cause—well, we'd had a little fight. Nothin' much. Just over somethin' I wanted. So I waited up. Yeah, with my hair all done up and my best nighty on."

"All right. So you waited up." Don tried to cover Miss Thalia's strangling gasp.

Cynthia shrugged and sat down. "Gimme a cigaret." As Don produced one and lit it she dragged deep, letting the smoke drift out with her words. "So I waited. Two, maybe three hours. He was talking to Luke till midnight, then someone else. I figured it was Franky."

"Franky Lund?"

She nodded. "Then I heard him leave and still Jake didn't come, so I figured he was really sore at me. Or maybe at her." She nodded disinterestedly at Miss Thalia. "You know what that old bat did to us today. In front of everybody. Sold us out on that Fund job—"

"Really!" Miss Thalia spluttered.

"Aw, button up. Maybe we asked for it. I don't know the in-fighting rules around this camp. Anyway, Jake was plenty burned up. Plenty. So I left him alone. I'm just about to give up, see, when I heard him laugh. Yeah, you could hear that bird laugh all the way up in my room. At first, I figure it's a mean laugh. Like he's got somebody over a barrel. Only it ain't. 'Cause I go to the head of the stairs and lean over, hoping I can see who it is he's got over a barrel. And I hear this yock. The real McCoy. I ain't heard him laugh like that since we come to this crummy town. Real laughing. I know it ain't Luke. He tells a gag like a guy readin' a Long Island timetable. And it ain't Lund, 'cause when he tells a story you don't hear the punch line for him laughing at it himself. This laugh is just Jake, letting go. So I come down to the front window and wait. I can see the hall or the yard from there, so I know I'll see who it is. Five, maybe ten minutes after that laugh, *she* goes home out the side door." Cynthia's voice went bleak. "Then I know."

The sudden end left Carol-Ann feeling that she'd pushed hard against a door that gave too easily. An empty-stomach feeling. Don urged Cynthia on. "And then what?"

"Nothin'." Cynthia shrugged. "I went upstairs. But couldn't sleep. I didn't even lie down." She sneered crookedly at Carol-Ann. "So I didn't muss my hair."

"Didn't you try to speak to Jake?"

"Oh, I tried the door but it was locked. And Jake didn't answer. So I went upstairs—till you came." Sudden, feverish anger burned in her eyes as she twisted around to glare at Carol-Ann. "You wanted it that way, baby. Now you got it. And you're stuck with it."

Obviously Cynthia was sincere—or a far better actress than Carol-Ann was willing to give her credit for. Undoubtedly she thought she had seen Carol-Ann in the dragon kimono. And that was what Carol-Ann had wanted to prove.

Don was looking at her perplexedly, as if to ask why she had insisted on putting herself on the spot. Even Miss Emily looked baffled, and Cassie stirred defensively. Carol-Ann took a deep breath. "I had to explain those footprints. At Miss Thalia's."

"She's confessing!" Cynthia came to life.

"Nuts. I'm just saying those footprints were there because my robe was out of place—or the other way round."

Cynthia blinked.

"It's perfectly simple. Where do you hang your bathrobe at night?" As Don hesitated, Carol-Ann nudged him. "You might as well tell me now as let me find out after we're married."

Don opened his mouth, closed it with a snap and then mumbled, "On the post at the foot of the bed."

"And you?" She aimed that directly at Cynthia.

"Me? Why, I . . . On the chest at the foot of the bed."

"How about you, Miss Emily?"

Miss Emily didn't get a chance to reply. Cassie cut in firmly. "On the back of that old rocker, like you seen a hunnert times." She bobbed her head sharply at Carol-

Ann. "And I flings mine on that old washstand so I can scoop it up quick does Miss Emily ring. Or go foragin'."

"And you, Miss Thalia?"

Miss Thalia made vague gestures in the air on either side of her, closing her eyes. "On my—throne." She opened her eyes and added hastily, "Not that I use it since we've had the bath installed. It's just always been there and I—"

"It's always been there!" Cynthia sneered. "That's Virginia!" She glanced at Carol-Ann. "So what's all this prove?"

"Probably nothing to you. Or the police. But a great deal to me. You see, you all know what you do with your bathrobes at night. It's a habit. I have one, too. I always drape mine over the back of a chair."

"So what?"

"I did it tonight. I even had to move a chair into place to put it on."

"So you moved a chair. You're a healthy girl."

"But the robe wasn't there when I woke up. It was flung over the foot of the bed."

Cynthia stared at her, waiting for something more. "What then? . . . Oh!"

"Yes. 'Oh!' . . . Somebody had used it. And put it back." Carol-Ann felt sure that was the reason the killer had worn those clumsy shoes across the garden—to return the robe without leaving identifiable footprints. To leave a robe— and pin a murder on her. Carol-Ann shivered. Only an accident had saved her—a small, seemingly unimportant accident. Now she had to prove that "accident."

Cynthia was frankly skeptical. "Who says it was moved? You. Who'd be nuts enough to swipe your robe and then take it back?"

"Who? I don't know. Why? Because it made a disguise. A very odd, very conspicuous disguise. And almost pinned a murder on me. It worked—almost. If your story is true."

"It's true enough. I seen that robe and—"

"And then you tried the doors of the den and they were locked."

"I tried 'em, and they were locked."

"After you'd seen my robe—leaving."

"After I seen *you* leaving."

"But, Cynthia, when we got here you and Don went to the den—and walked right in."

"So Jake unlocked the doors."

"After you saw my robe leaving? Remember, you saw it leave before you tried the doors and found them locked."

"What of it? Jake coulda got up and—" Cynthia's stylized face crumpled. "He couldn'ta. He was dead. He . . . You came back!" She whirled at Carol-Ann, fingers raking the air. "You came back!"

"There wasn't time. Miss Thalia screamed when she saw somebody at her window—and I've had an alibi ever since. No, Cynthia, I find I like your story of seeing 'me' and my robe very much. Very much indeed. Because it means I couldn't possibly have killed Jake."

"I don't get it." Cynthia shook her head as if to clear it.

"Somebody must have been in the den after you saw 'me' leave—somebody who unlocked the doors into the house."

For a long moment Cynthia sat there, and then the full meaning of Carol-Ann's words sank in. She stiffened. "Into the house? Look, are you saying . . ." Her words hung up there as if she were trying to straighten them out for herself.

"I'm only saying that after you saw me leave, somebody unlocked those doors. If it was Jake, he was still alive—after you saw me leave. If it was somebody else . . ." Carol-Ann shrugged. "There's the murderer. And I have an alibi. So I really like your story. Or are you planning to change it again?"

"I—" Cynthia turned her face up to Don, her hand raised appealingly. "I did see her leave. And I did find the door locked. So I couldn't have gone in. I . . ." She dropped her head in her hands. "I loved the lug."

12

Don managed to calm Cynthia down enough to get some sense out of her. "What time did you hear Jake laugh and come downstairs?"

Cynthia sulked in her chair, crouching away from the light. "I don't know. But that old clock in the hall struck two-thirty when I seen her." She turned to glower at Carol-Ann. "And I still think it was her leaving."

"Did you see her—or anyone—come back?"

Cynthia seemed to debate that for a long moment and then shook her head. "Naw. I didn't wait. I went upstairs."

"After trying the door of the den."

"Yeah. Only it's not really a lock. Just a knob. Latch, sort of. You can't open it except from inside."

"And you went up to bed?"

"Yeah. Only I couldn't sleep. I—I— Well, I was sore at that dame. I just kinda roamed around my room. Waiting for Jake."

"And you stayed until you heard us knocking?" At Cynthia's disinterested nod he went on. "Did you hear anything else? Anyone moving around? A door open?"

"I was so burned up I . . ." Cynthia pressed her fingers against her forehead. "I—I don't know. I don't remember nothing like that. I just know I kept thinking it took Jake a helluva time to lock up."

Miss Emily shifted her weight forward, leaning on her stick. "Then you heard sounds you thought were Jake locking up?"

"I don't know."

"Was it a dead silence?"

"Oh! No, I guess not, or I'd have . . . Yeah. Then maybe I did hear something. I get what you mean." She tilted her face up to Don. "She came back." It had become a theme song, a chorus.

Don shook his head. "Impossible. Miss Marsten saw her asleep then went downstairs. Miss Emily heard her scream and phoned the police. That's timed at two-forty. Officially. Miss Foster was with Miss Marsten almost immediately after she screamed and has been in the presence of two or more people ever since."

"Well," Cynthia seemed resigned that her great exposé had come to nothing, "I can't figure it. It looks like whoever swiped your robe didn't kill Jake, seein' as somebody unlocked that door later."

She sat up straight. "Or maybe Jake did it himself—to let somebody in. He coulda."

"Almost anything could have happened. The one thing we know couldn't have happened is that Miss Foster couldn't have been the person you saw wearing the robe. From there on it's wide open."

Luke stepped into the room. "I hear your men outside."

Don nodded. "They have their instructions."

"I wish to be present when they open that room."

Don smiled faintly. "Have you been standing guard at the door all this time?"

"Young man," Luke's voice went high and he fought it down, "there should be quite a sum of money in that room. I find nothing amusing about sixty thousand dollars."

"None of us thinks this is a bit amusing. There's also a dead man in that room. Your partner. We don't think that's funny. And most likely he didn't, either." Don blinked at his own words, studied them almost as if they hung in the air before him. "And yet he may have died laughing."

"What's that? What's that?"

Miss Emily clasped both hands over the knob of her stick and rested several of her chins on them. "He doesn't know it yet, but he may have said something very sensible. Time and the coroner will tell."

Luke's thin, bloodless lips sneered at Miss Emily. "Was that intended to be cryptic?"

"Cryptic, nothing! Downright flabbergasting." Miss Emily brooded on it darkly. "And maybe disconcerting. And if it's true, maybe we've got an ear-witness to a murder."

"That sounds extremely clever, Mrs. Tilworthy. Perhaps it means something. But right now that locked door is bothering me."

"Bothering *you?* It's driving me nuts. Only I don't think we're talking about the same locked door. Or do I mean the same door but locked at different times?"

Don put his hand to his head. "Don't say things like that. You're just complicating it. It couldn't be like that."

Luke peered from one to the other, glaring. "Like what?"

Miss Emily concentrated on Don, ignoring Luke. "Either it's like that, or Cynthia Scudder is the most accomplished liar I've ever encountered. And you should arrest her for murder.

"Stop persecuting my sister!"

Carol-Ann, intent on the puzzling attunement between Don and Miss Emily, whipped her head around to see Andy Stevens shouldering Luke aside, the tasseled belt of his robe tight around him. The deep mauve brocade, the wide satin revers, the sash belt with its outsized white tassels should have made him look jaunty and debonair. Instead, the mauve tone and the shiny revers only accented the sallowness of his skin and the puffiness around his eyes that might have come from recent sleep. Certainly he strove to give an impression of just awakening. He rubbed his eyes. He yawned elaborately before he hurried over to take Cynthia's hand. "Are these guys getting rough with my little sister?"

Cynthia tugged her hand away, obviously astonished at this display of brotherly affection. "Are you looped again?" She caught his outstretched hand. "Let me smell your breath."

"Aw, Sis . . ." He wriggled free, resuming his man-of-affairs pose. "Are they bothering you, kid?"

Cynthia frowned, looked at Miss Emily, at Carol-Ann and finally up at Don, honestly perplexed. "I don't think so. But something funny is going on around here, and I got a feeling I'm elected patsy."

"Not while I'm around, Sis."

That seemed to wake Cynthia from her bemused puzzlement. "And how come you're around? When did you get in?"

"Me?" Andy cinched his belt tighter. "Came in with Franky. I was at the club and he told me he was going to see Jake, so I tagged along, thinking maybe it was about . . . thinking I could help Jake out on the deal. Only it was all set." He looked down at his nails. "They didn't need me, so I went to bed."

"You been here all this time?"

"Yeah." Andy yawned. "I was dead tired. Hard day."

"You were here? I didn't—" Cynthia began and he caught her hand in both of his.

"Don't try to talk, baby. Just relax. This has been a shock. I'll handle these guys. After all, I'm head of the house now."

Don tapped his shoulder. "That could be. But how did you know? Dream about it?"

Andy released Cynthia's hand and smiled slyly. "Trying to trap me? I heard it from those goons of yours you've got trampling up the evidence in the garden."

Don flushed, knotting his fists. "They're pretty smart boys, Stevens, and they don't trample evidence. But what makes you think there'd be evidence in the garden?"

Andy shifted uneasily. "Because they're trampling."

"If there's evidence there, they'll find it. Right now we're looking for footprints."

Andy's eyes narrowed thoughtfully. "Footprints?" He shrugged. "You'll find mine. I'm in and out through that office door a dozen times a day. After all, this is my home." He shrugged some imaginary wrinkle out of the robe. "My home," he repeated softly, his eyes roved, appraising each piece. "You'll find my prints out there. Among others."

"Not so many others, fortunately." Miss Emily offered. "Not many others."

"No?" A flicker of surprise ran under Andy's puffy lids, but his voice was still bantering. "Everybody uses that door. Even tradesmen."

"But not since five o'clock when I saw Aaron—or was it Moses—raking the garden."

Andy's teetering stopped in midteeter and he sank back on his heels. "So they'll still find my footprints. That's the shortest way to the garage. And come to think of it, I stepped out for a smoke while Jake and Franky were talking."

"So we should find three sets of your footprints? Two going and one returning?" Don made the question sound casual.

"Or maybe more. I don't stand around like a moron when I'm smoking."

"No?" Miss Emily suppressed a yawn. "When do you stand around like a moron?"

"Cyn," Andy ignored Miss Emily, pulled her to her feet, "I think you should get some rest." He tried to make his gaze on Don direct and forceful. "If you don't mind."

Don waved them out of the room and turned to Luke. "The men are about through. I've no objection to your being present when we search the room. You might even be able to help. Know the combination of the safe?"

"Jake and I were partners. You will find my fingerprints on it." He gave Don the frosty beginnings of a smile. "Legitimately." He led the way down the hall.

"Miss Emily," Cassie's rich voice was tinged with worry. "Yestiddy was Thursday, ain't it? I mean, even if we ain't had no sleep yet, yestiddy was Thursday and this yere is gonna be Friday?"

"Yes, Cassie."

"Well, Thursday is Aaron's day to work, an' you know he got the burst-itis." She explained this cryptic statement to Don. "Aaron and Mose is twins, and one of 'em works one day and the other the next. Moses on Mondays, Wednesdays and Fridays, and Aaron Tuesdays, Thursdays and Sat'days—and they both rests Sundays. And they don't never swap around."

Miss Emily agreed. "And Aaron has bursitis."

"Well," Cassie was troubled, "he couldn't been doin' no gardenin' yestiddy afternoon and raked up no footprints. And it ain't Moses' day."

"It may turn out this hasn't been Andy's day, either." Miss Emily levered herself up and patted Cassie's shoulder. "It's all right. We didn't do any gardening, either, but I think we raked up some facts."

13

"Our friend Andy Stevens was most anxious to establish that his footprints might be found outside the door to the garden, and Luke Snedicker wasn't very far behind in setting up the possible presence of his fingerprints on the safe." Don winked at Miss Emily and started out. He turned back for a slow, studious scrutiny of Carol-Ann, setting her to a very pleasant tingling.

Carol-Ann hugged herself lightly and grinned at Miss Emily. "At least the idea is beginning to seep in."

Miss Emily wriggled uncomfortably. "Don's not stupid enough to believe that razzle-dazzle for long."

Carol-Ann stared at Miss Emily, searching carefully for a sign of humor, but the rugged old face was grim. "Razzle-dazzle?"

"About the robe. And you being sound asleep and having an alibi."

"But I was asleep. And I do have an alibi."

"For what?"

"Why, for Jake's murder."

"Do you? You have an alibi for the time after Cynthia saw somebody in the robe leaving. Just because she found the door locked then—and unlocked later, we've assumed Jake was alive after the robe left—and his murderer unlocked the door."

"Well, yes. Either Jake was alive to unlock it—or his murderer did." Carol-Ann was horrified. "It has to be that way. If somebody had gone in there and found him dead, they'd have phoned the police, not just unlocked the door and—" She broke off uncertainly. "But why would anyone?"

"I can think of sixty thousand reasons."

"Lund's money!" Carol-Ann tried to imagine what sixty thousand dollars would mean to her but found she couldn't think in those terms. It was just an incredible amount of money. "But steal from a dead man!"

"I imagine that would be the only safe way to steal from Jake, after he was dead. The killer and the door unlocker don't have to be the same person."

Carol-Ann stared down at the gay colors of her robe. "And it could have been the murderer who walked away—in my robe." She held it away from her body distastefully.

"Not necessarily." For all her bulk Miss Emily could leap nimbly from one side of an argument to the other. "The robe wearer may have had nothing to do with the murder. It may be somebody's idea of a practical joke. Or an attempt to make Cynthia jealous. Andy could easily have tried something like that. It's obvious he depends for his living in keeping Sister Dear under his thumb. Anyway, nobody has proved yet that Jake was dead when the robe left here, no matter who was in it."

Carol-Ann shivered. "But he didn't answer Cynthia's knock."

"That doesn't mean he was dead. I can think of a dozen reasons not to answer, including the one that he just didn't want to talk to Cynthia—which would be perfectly understandable in my book. Or he may have had someone in there he didn't want Cynthia to see. Jake may have unlocked the door himself, after Cynthia went upstairs. And even let in a third person and been killed several minutes later."

"Then my robe . . ." Carol-Ann inspected it intently, as if she expected it to yield new clues.

"Your robe may have nothing to do with the murder. The unlocking of that door seems to eliminate you—and your robe—from the murder."

"It's missing." Don stood in the archway looking tired. Carol-Ann wanted to run to him, to touch his weary, grim face. Then she wondered how long he'd stood there, listening.

Miss Emily nodded as if she had expected him. "Was there ever any money?"

"Lund says there was. I just talked to him. He says he has Jake's receipt. Not for sixty thousand, though. Forty-two."

"Why, Jake paid Judge Bo that much for the place and he must have spent as much more on restoration." Carol-Ann scowled past Don into the darkened hall. "Jake must have hated us all, to sell that cheap, just to hurt us with a gambling den."

"I guess he did. He had a pretty shabby trick played on him. In public."

"Well!" Miss Thalia gasped, fluffing thin hand at her ruffles. "Well, I must say I never expected any such criticism." She almost sprang from her chair, shaking herself into her frilly robe. "I did what was right and necessary. The very idea of that man trying to push himself and that woman into our social set. Why, he was just a common contractor. I'll not stay another minute under this roof. I shall return to my own home."

"Certainly, Miss Marsten. I'll send someone with you." Don smiled with all but his eyes. "Of course, it will have to be just a common policeman."

He came back from seeing her and the common policeman out and sagged wearily against the archway. "Miss

Emily, I've been looking at you for two nights straight now. Couldn't you go home and go to bed?" He relieved the impertinence of it with a tired grin. "Too many things happen when you're around. Goofy things. Somebody robs a house to steal a postcard nobody can read anyway. Footprints leap into windows and stop in the middle of a room. Robes vanish and unvanish. Doors lock and unlock. Money appears and disappears."

"That's what I want to hear about." Miss Emily obviously had no intention of departing until she had heard. "Everybody agrees that Jake was going to get sixty thousand dollars, and he never struck me as being a man who'd take less than he bargained for."

"I don't think he did. Lund claimed his receipt was for forty-two thousand cash and 'other valuable considerations,' which he didn't care to explain."

"Or didn't dare to?"

"Go home and go to bed. I can't afford to be that bright at four in the morning. I don't even want to guess it was for gambling debts. Lund's coming in at two tomorrow—for the preliminary hearing. You might be there. You, too, Miss Foster. Just to help confuse the coroner thoroughly. No need of doing things halfway. That robe—I wish I'd never seen it."

Don scrubbed his left temple wearily with his knuckles. "The robe wearer and the door unlocker were probably separate people—and Mrs. Scudder heard Jake laughing before the robe wearer left. The door unlocker came later. So it seems more likely he's the killer than the one with whom Jake was enjoying a good laugh. So I'm not so interested in the robe."

Doctor Dolman walked in from the darkened hall. Don turned to him immediately.

"How'd it go, Doc?"

Doctor Dolman's face was a puzzle. "Tell more after I get at him." He held his hands out. "I'll look for strychnine—or aconite."

"Poison? Jake Scudder was poisoned?" Don straightened slowly, glaring at the doctor. "Poison!"

Doctor Dolman turned his hands over and inspected the palms, frowning. "Nicotine, strychnine, aconite. Aconite's rare."

Carol-Ann stared at the doctor. He was getting fog-minded. Hadn't he seen the knife in Jake's back?

"Not prussic acid. No characteristic peachstone odor. No cynanosis, either." The doctor scowled. He knotted his hands into fists and jammed them into his pockets. "But the rictus is present. Quite pronounced."

Don took a deep breath and turned back to the doctor. "But the knife—"

Doctor Dolman nodded abstractedly. "The knife. Yes. The knife." He heaved a sigh. "Undoubtedly the immediate cause of death. It snapped a vertebra, penetrating the heart."

"It can't be poison!" Don protested. "It's impossible!"

The doctor allowed himself a shallow smile. "You've got poison—or something else just as impossible. We can't get around that rictus. So you can take your choice. Poison or . . ." he shook his head at the manifest absurdity . . . "you have a man who enjoyed being killed. At least he died laughing."

He died laughing!

That meant the robe had played its part in murder. Carol-Ann felt suddenly chilled in the hot summer night and huddled herself together.

14

After an almost directed verdict of "death at the hands of person or persons unknown" the coroner's jury of four farmers, a school principal and a mechanic was dismissed with thanks, and they all filed uneasily out. No mention had been made of the unaccountable footprints, the robe, or the door. Don had forewarned Carol-Ann not to expect them. Those items were being saved for presentation to the Grand Jury, if and when they had anyone to indict.

Miss Emily, emerging from the warmth of the court-room into the cool shadows of late afternoon, braced her-self with her stick, sneezed violently once and summed up the whole proceedings succinctly. "Well, they proved Jake Scudder is dead, and I knew that last night." But there was more than that.

Doctor Dolman, after an autopsy, had abandoned any idea of poison and had accepted the other impossible—that the rictus was just what it seemed—death laughter. Jake had died laughing.

Carol-Ann had gotten that much out of the tangle of medical language. Jake Scudder had been stabbed in the middle of a laugh, and the knife had penetrated between two vertebrae and severed the spinal cord, causing instan-taneous paralysis and near-instantaneous death. He had died laughing.

Even in the afternoon warmth Carol-Ann shivered. Though it hadn't been mentioned, there was still Cynthia's story that she had heard Jake's bellow of laughter and later seen the blue-and-gold robe leaving. Coupled with Doctor Dolman's findings, that made the robe uncomfortably prominent. Yet Cynthia's own story of the lock-unlocked door made it a greater enigma. And nobody had yet adequately explained the unfinished footsteps.

Out of the corner of her eye she saw a little man arguing persuasively and maybe a little furtively with Ronnie.

"I beg your pardon." Andy spoke softly behind her and she wheeled to face a crooked, loose smile and eyes that slithered over her quickly and back to her face. "About the robe business . . ." He smiled nastily. "There's another witness." Before Carol-Ann could speak he moved in and pinioned her arm against his side. "And I think you and I had better discuss it. Privately. I've got my car. We can have dinner at the Pine Tree Inn and then—" he smirked—"talk."

Carol-Ann had been too astonished to do more than stare at the man's sallow face and watch his thick, poutish lips construct words. Now she tugged her arm to free it, but he caught her wrist.

"I wouldn't be hasty. This witness might say some very damaging things about who wore a certain robe . . ." Andy shrugged lightly and squeezed on her wrist. "Or he might be persuaded . . ." He shrugged again, smirking. "After all, we're friends."

"You have friends?"

His sallow face flushed and his hand tightened convulsively on Carol-Ann's. "Sure I have friends. Lots of friends. And when I get through, I'm gonna have lots more friends. Like you and me are gonna be friends."

It was incredible. It couldn't be happening. Carol-Ann looked down at her arm tucked through his, felt the hot, moist pressure of his hand around her wrist. She couldn't even quite comprehend what he was saying, yet she saw the ugliness with which he said it. "You're hurting me." It seemed such a stupid thing to say but she couldn't dredge up other words. In a moment, she knew, she would react. With genuine comprehension would come anger. She was even beginning to swing her free hand for a good stinging blow across his slack mouth.

"Hanging hurts worse." Andy seemed to find this very funny. He repeated it, chuckling. "Hanging hurts worse." As if that had cleared up the whole murky situation, he started forward, dragging on Carol-Ann's arm, when Miss Emily's bulk barred their way.

Andy scowled but he didn't release Carol-Ann's arm. She could feel him tense as he tried to tug her to one side. "Let's go, baby. We got a date."

Miss Emily's smile was almost amiable. "I just can't help overhearing things. Especially when I try." She smiled wisely. "You should be careful about seizing opportunities too easily handed you. It can lead to trouble. Such as you're in now."

"Me?" Andy laughed uneasily.

"You. So you know a witness who is willing to swear that Carol-Ann was leaving Jake's den at two-thirty last night?"

"Did I say so?" Andy attempted another move around Miss Emily, tugging at Carol-Ann, who had relaxed to watch Miss Emily's maneuver. It was simple. She merely stepped in front of Andy. "But this character can be persuaded he saw somebody else." Andy tried a smile that slipped. "If I do the persuading. . ."

Miss Emily turned half around and let loose a bellow that jerked heads around all over the courthouse green. "Don! Come here!"

Andy glared. "That was stupid." He released Carol-Ann's arm and started to run. Miss Emily's stick whipped out, went neatly between his legs, and he plowed into the gravel with a surprised grunt.

Don looked down at Andy. He didn't offer to help him up.

"She knocked me down," Andy complained and winced at someone's laughter.

Don glanced at Miss Emily for explanation.

"I don't like him because of the way he parts his hair."

Andy groaned, rolled over and sat up, running his hand uncertainly over the crew cut he hoped made him look youthful.

Don twinkled at Miss Emily. "He doesn't part his hair."

"Pick three other reasons." Miss Emily prodded at the sprawling man with the detached curiosity of a man poking a strange insect. "And then arrest him for attempted extortion."

Carol-Ann saw the tightening muscles in Don's jaw, the clenching of his fists. "Did he threaten Carol-Ann?"

"Hey!" Andy was alarmed. "What's the harm in asking a girl to dinner?"

"You." Miss Emily looked down at him and sighed, delivering him over to Don. "But I suppose the only thing you can really take him in for is questioning. He claims to know a witness to the Scudder murder."

Somewhere in the crowd behind her Carol-Ann heard a gasp, but she turned too late to see who it was. She did, however, see Cynthia elbowing her way to the front, staring down in horrid fascination at her brother. Ronnie, coming up behind her, tried to stop her but she shook off his hand and stepped forward. Through the momentary gap she left Carol-Ann could see Judge Bo thrusting haughtily at the little man who said something he evidently thought devastating.

Don had Andy on his feet by the time Cynthia reached him, her face cold and hard.

"Look, jerk, what's the beef?"

Don shoved Andy forward. "He has just—er—volunteered some information about a witness to your husband's murder."

"Oh!" She stood frozen a moment, glaring at Don; then her eyes raked Andy. Carol-Ann could feel her cold animosity, but whether it was for Don or her brother she couldn't tell. Abruptly Cynthia turned and stalked off toward the big Cadillac, brushing aside Ronnie's gesture of assistance.

15

Carol-Ann was digesting Miss Emily's baked ham, candied yams and fruit salad drowned pleasantly in a French dressing made with sour wine, and a wedge of chess pie on crumbly cheese pastry. Lazily she tried to decide between fashion and the comfort that would come of undoing the gold clasps of her belt. She decided that if Don could handle that extra slice of chess pie without unbuttoning his Trooper's tunic, she could endure the belt.

Miss Emily suffered from no such constrictions. She waved a forkful of pie at Don. "When Cassie's upset, she always outdoes herself cooking, so I know better than to wear my girdle."

"Is Cassie upset?" Don pushed his empty pie plate closer.

"Murder upsets some people. Have some more pie?"

"Actually I suppose I shouldn't be eating socially with a suspect." He grinned at Carol-Ann.

The pie got suddenly heavy in Carol-Ann's stomach. "Am I a suspect?"

"Not to me. Even without Miss Thalia's alibi for you. But Andy Stevens has tried to make out a case, mostly to spite Miss Emily, I think. But once we get hold of this witness of his—Willie Earps—we should clear up the whole case."

"Willie Earps?" Miss Emily scowled. "Do I know him?"

"Maybe. He's that little man who hangs around the courthouse. Peddles tax titles, searches for title flaws and sells the information to whoever will buy it."

"Oh, him." Carol-Ann frowned. "Who would?"

"Buy from him? You might, if he turned up a flaw in the title to your property. The information should be worth something, just so you could correct it. It's a form of blackmail; it keeps him from turning it over to someone else."

"He sounds squirmy."

"I'm not worried about his character; it's his eyesight. Who or what did he see outside Jake's last night. If he was there. If he saw anything."

"And Andy tried to use that just to get a date with me?"

"He's cured of that as a method." Don cut savagely through his third piece of pie.

"Did he sound as if he really knew who Earps saw? If he saw anybody?"

Don studied the last bite of pie, not really seeing it. He stabbed at it violently. "He says not. But he's scared. And I can't figure out if he's scared we won't find Willie—and leave him with a hole in his story. Or scared we will find him and maybe leave Andy with no story at all. And I can't figure out why Earps would be hanging around Jake's at that hour, anyway."

"Could be he was trying one of his tricks on Jake."

"That wouldn't have been healthy—and it was Jake who died."

"Could Earps have killed him?"

Don started to say no and then nodded. "Physically, yes, even if he is a runt. It wasn't much of a blow, and the doc figures most of the force came from Jake when he threw himself back, laughing. Almost accidental murder, you might say. But if he did kill Jake, I don't see him telling Andy about it afterward. Not even telling him he was around." Don paused. "Or did he? Or did Andy see him there?"

"Andy was asleep. Remember?"

"I remember Andy gave a good demonstration of just waking up but I also noticed Mrs. Scudder wasn't so ready to buy it. Our Andy could easily have been up and around." Don puzzled over it for a moment. "I'm glad we've got him locked up. Once we confront him with Earps—"

"Could Earps have been peddling some title flaw to Jake?"

"Scudder wasn't buying any property."

"He bought the land for the Memorial."

"And gave it away. A flaw in that title would worry him like a hole in somebody else's sock."

"He bought Judge Bo's place."

"That's been in the Tayloe family for two hundred years. From an original grant. There couldn't be a flaw." Don pondered for a moment. "Or could there? Anyway, we'll know as soon as we find Earps." He stood up with only a slight effort and made his goodbyes. "I've got to get back on the job, but first I've got a messy duty." He appealed to Carol-Ann. "That's what I really came over for. Will you help? She's likely to have hysterics." He shuddered. "And when that woman has hysterics, she has 'em high, wide and loathsome."

"Who? I mean, of course I'll help. But who? About what?"

"Miss Marsten. I've got to break it to her that the Coast Guard have proof her brother was murdered. Thank the Lord that case is out of my territory."

Miss Emily laid down her fork, staring at him. "Ted Marsten? Murdered? He didn't have an enemy in the world. Most inoffensive man that ever lived."

"Murdered. And robbed. Of nine thousand dollars."

"Ridiculous. Ted hasn't seen nine thousand dollars in that many days."

"He had it in Charleston. In cash. New bills. Mostly fifties. Just before he sailed for Albemarle Sound. He bought gas on the Intracoastal Waterways with one of the bills. It's been identified."

"A lugger doesn't use gas." Miss Emily seemed to be arguing against her own slowly dawning realization of murder.

"His does. It has an auxiliary kicker. He uses it in the canals."

"I remember now." Miss Emily rose tiredly. "Poor Thalia. This is going to be a shock because I don't think she even fully realizes yet that he's dead. She shuts herself away from realities." Miss Emily shook herself firmly and reached for her stick. "I'll go talk to Thalia. You go find that Willie Earps."

They all heard the stifled squawk, the sudden, rattling roar of an old car motor, tires screaming in sudden torture and then the crash, the splintering of wood, the tinny crunch of metal, the tinkle of breaking glass.

Another highway crash! Then Carol-Ann realized it was closer. Right outside. In front of Miss Emily's. Before she could get herself moving Don had hurtled past her and out the door, with Miss Emily close behind.

Carol-Ann could see the wreck from the porch. Headlights of a car canted drunkenly against the picket enclosure for trash at the corner of the yard. Lights streamed out in a curiously cross-eyed way through the pines.

As she reached the tilted side of the old Ford, Don backed through the open door and blocked her way with spread arms, but not before she had seen the pinched rabbity face of the little man at the courthouse.

They had found Willie Earps. And he was dead.

16

Carol-Ann sat in Cynthia's synthetic gloom and shivered, only partially hearing Don's words as he questioned Luke and Cynthia.

Willie Earps was dead with an icepick through his neck. The best assumption at the moment was that he had been talking to his killer with his foot on the Ford's clutch, either because he was merely impatient to get going or because he had anticipated some sort of assault and was in readiness for a quick getaway. He hadn't made it. The icepick had gone in, and Willie had flung up both hands to fight this horror in his throat, and his foot had let up on the clutch. The Ford had surged forward and crashed into Miss Emily's picket-framed trash enclosure, almost a trade mark of this country section of Virginia Beach.

Gradually, as if both eyes and mind were adjusting to the gloom, Carol-Ann could make out Cynthia sitting in rigid defiance in the low, modern chair, her hands under control but her eyes jerking away from Don's face to scan the room in twitching little hops that didn't seem to see anything, then return to Don's face. Luke perched on a stiff straight chair and somehow managed to look relaxed, like a man who had accompanied a friend to the dentist, solemnly aware that there was pain and grief but basically pleased it wasn't for him.

"And neither of you has an alibi," Don concluded his summation.

Cynthia stirred, fastening her eyes on Don's face. "I was in my boudoir—and a lady don't have alibis in her boudoir. I don't know where Luke was. He says—"

Don inclined his head toward Snedicker. "He's quite capable of telling it himself."

"The first point is, do we—or do I—need an alibi?" Luke tapped his fingers together and then spread them eloquently. "I think not. To the best of my knowledge I never knew any Willie Earps."

"You don't have to know the name and address of a witness to a murder to know you have to get rid of him." Don rubbed his jaw thoughtfully. "But you did know him. You were seen talking to him at the courthouse today. In the corridor. He stopped you. He had a briefcase."

"Oh, that man. . . ." Luke tented his fingers, scowling. "Was that Willie Earps? He was trying to sell me something. But then, isn't everybody?" He said it with complete disillusionment. "I didn't buy."

"I wish you had. You might have bought Jake's murderer—and Willie's life."

"Aren't you assuming rather much?"

"No. I have Andy Stevens' word—rather reluctantly given—that Earps could identify Jake's murderer. I think Earps came by here to look you people over and check up." Don said it so casually that the real meaning almost escaped Carol-Ann. Had Earps believed one of them was guilty. Had he? And died because of it?

Luke apparently didn't get the implication for he went right on. "Or he came out of morbid curiosity. Have you any idea how many cars have passed down this street today? Normally it's a quiet side street."

"I know precisely how many cars have passed down this street. Every one is being checked. Particularly those that came by more than once." Don grinned wryly down at Snedicker. "Incidentally, you have neatly talked your way around your own alibi. Where were you from eight-thirty to nine?"

Snedicker shrugged. "If you mean a corroborated alibi—I haven't one. I was going over papers in Jake's den when I heard the crash. I don't customarily read confidential papers before an audience."

Don nodded glumly and was about to say something more when a scuffling in the hall interrupted him. He swung around.

Even before she heard Miss Thalia's stifled squeak of dismay Carol-Ann recognized Judge Bo's indignant face as he twitched and twisted in a Trooper's grip. Once in the room the Trooper released him. "This one of the guys you wanted?" At Don's nod the Trooper saluted again. "Caught him sneaking through that yard—"

Judge Bo shook himself back into a semblance of dignity. "I must protest the indignity of this arrest."

"It wasn't an arrest," Don began.

Judge Bo ignored that. "I was not sneaking. I had an appointment with Miss Marsten and—"

"Oh, dear!" Miss Thalia wailed softly. "I forgot. When I heard the crash I just flew—over to Emily's. Oh, Beauregard, please forgive me."

Judge Bo bowed perplexedly into the gloom, in the general direction of Miss Thalia's voice. "Of course, Thalia. Most certainly I forgive you." He turned to plant himself firmly before Don. "And now I'd like an explanation of this indignity."

Miss Emily's voice boomed out. "I'll assure 'em, Bo. Only that's not the trouble. A man was killed."

Judge Bo gasped in horror and turned to look back down the hall. "In that wreck? I noticed it as this man was arresting—"

"It was not an arrest, Judge Tayloe," Don explained patiently. "I simply asked our man to get you and several others up for questioning."

"Oh!" Judge Bo studied that a moment. "Then why aren't you questioning me?"

"I'm trying to." Don said it with dogged patience. "Did you know Willie Earps?"

Judge Bo nodded brightly. "Yes. A most obnoxious little man. Most obnoxious. Do you know what he tried to do? He said that in his research—he has the audacity to call his fumbling among court papers 'research'—he had learned that William Butler Tayloe—the grandson of the original Signer—had once wagered the title to Holly Hall on a horse race!"

"Flaw in the title . . ." Don murmured almost to himself. "And I said there couldn't be one." He spoke up, directly to Judge Bo. "Then how did the family get it back?"

Judge Bo looked at him blankly. "Get it back? We never lost it."

"But you said he wagered the title on a horse race."

"Oh, that! He won it!"

"He did?"

"Naturally. The Tayloe horses were quite famous." Judge Bo's assurance was so complete that Don had to stifle a smile.

"Then why should Earps tell you about it?"

"Oh, he asked a small price for his silence."

"Did you pay him?"

"Ridiculous! Of course not. Why should I? It's a tradition!"

"So that's what Willie Earps was talking to you about this afternoon."

"Oh, no. That was months ago."

Don sighed resignedly. "What was Willie talking to you about this afternoon?"

"He offered to sell me some information he claimed would get my home back for me. Or so I gathered. He was vague. A flaw in the deed, I gathered."

Cynthia gasped. "There was not! Jake bought me that house fair and square."

Don ignored her. "Did you buy that, Judge?"

Judge Bo looked at Don incredulously. "Why should I? I should most certainly have had to pay back the purchase money, and I've already spent some of it." He paused dreamily. "On a perfect little house. Absolutely perfect. Modern. Ranch style, I believe they call it. Most amazing. Heated by panels in the walls. And a most utilitarian kitchen. Truly a delight. A dishwasher and something that gets rid of garbage and—"

Don almost glared at the little man. "But just yesterday you were trying to prevent Scudder from selling your home."

"That is quite different." Judge Bo lost his air of childish delight in his cottage and drew himself into dignity. "I couldn't permit him to sell the Tayloe home for a gambling den. Gambling is—iniquitous."

"But—" Don looked bewildered. "You just said your great-grandfather, or somebody, bet the house on a horse race. And you were proud of it."

Judge Bo snorted. "Sir, there is considerable difference between a gentlemanly wager and gambling."

"Oh, sure." Don gave up and went back to essentials.

"But if you wanted to prevent Lund from opening it as a gambling house, why didn't you accept Earps' offer?"

"It was unnecessary. Emily had assured me of another way to prevent it."

Don hurriedly continued, "So Willie Earps meant very little to you?"

"Less than nothing, I assure you. Except that I dislike the type." Judge Bo shuddered gently.

"Did he tell you he was a witness to Scudder's murder?"

"Was he? Oh, dear, no, he didn't tell me, but I can't think why he would. Can you?"

Don sighed. "No, and I don't know that he was." When Judge Bo looked blankly perplexed, Don hurried on. "Where were you between eight-thirty and nine?"

"Is it important?" As Don nodded Judge Bo contemplated the ceiling. "We dined at seven, which means we finished somewhere around quarter to eight. Then I had my post-prandial cigar. That usually takes about twenty to twenty-five minutes. So at eight-fifteen, I'd say, I started for Miss Marsten's. To pay my respects."

"He was getting up nerve to propose to Thalia," whispered Miss Emily.

"So perhaps it was eight-forty, or eight-forty-five, possibly even later when I arrived at Miss Marsten's residence. I rang the bell, waited some few moments, rang it again— and eventually became aware of the commotion across the yards and came over to investigate. That is when your man apprehended me."

"Uh-huh. So you were alone right up to the time my man spotted you."

"Oh, not entirely. Ronnie Parker was with me at dinner."

"Ronnie?" Cynthia's voice skirled off into querulousness. "Ronnie had dinner at *your* house?"

"He does quite often. Interesting young man. Clever. Quite ingenious. He's rooming with me." Judge Bo smiled rather shyly. "I expect I bore him a bit, but we get along."

Cynthia gawped at the Judge and then invited the room at large to witness this unbelievable situation—Jake Scudder's nephew accepted as a guest by a genuine, authenticated F.F.V.

Don squelched any further social aspirations. "So you and Ronnie were together? How long?"

Judge Bo considered. "Until I left for my walk. Ronnie was coming over here for his things and offered to drive, but I felt I should really enjoy the walk."

"Then you don't have an alibi for the time Willie Earps was killed?"

"Willie Earps? Killed?" Judge Bo peered again toward the front door. "In that wreck out there?"

"Something like that," Don admitted.

Judge Bo turned back. "How dreadful! Even for a nasty little man like him." Then he smiled almost gayly at Don. "But you see, I couldn't possibly have killed him."

"No?"

"No. You see, I don't drive a car. Oh, dear, that's how he died, isn't it?"

"Not exactly. He was stabbed with an icepick."

Don turned Judge Bo toward the corner where Miss Thalia sat and gave him a little shove. Judge Bo went meekly and sat in whispered conference with Miss Thalia while Don went outside. Carol-Ann had many questions. Most of those she wanted to ask, only the dead man could have answered. And perhaps he was dead because he was the only person who could.

No, there was one question that didn't need Willie— what was the flaw in Jake's deed to Holly Hall? The flaw must still be there, even though Earps was dead. There must be something to it, for that would explain Earps' presence near the house on the night of the murder. He could have been there trying to sell that information to Jake. She felt she ought to point this out to Don and had half risen from her chair when Miss Emily's hand thrust her back.

"Let him alone. He's doing all right. He can figure that's why Earps was here last night."

That was the disconcerting part of Miss Emily. You almost forgot she was hearing the same things—and coming up with nearly identical answers—or maybe even a little better as she proceeded to demonstrate.

"Or he can be figuring Willie saw Frankie Lund—after he'd paid Jake—and told him the deed had a flaw. It's the sort of thing Willie seemed to enjoy doing, if he could make a dollar at it. And then Willie could have waited around, watching the house for results."

"You mean Willie may have egged Lund into going back and demanding his money—and Lund killed Jake in the argument? And took his money back?"

"It doesn't sound like Lund." Miss Emily had thought over Carol-Ann's last statement. "Big time gamblers hire their murders done. This one is too—accidental?—subtle? Accidental? It could be that. Lund may not have started out to murder Jake, but even if he had, in a rage, I'm sure he'd have taken care of a witness like Earps differently."

"The money is gone. . . ."

"Anybody with sticky fingers could have taken it. The theft could have been the motive—and Willie just got in the way." Miss Emily thumped her stick in exasperation, her voice rising. "And Ted's murder fits in somewhere. It must—"

A high wail assailed them, and Miss Thalia lunged from her chair. "Not Ted! Ted wasn't murdered. He died on his boat—" Miss Thalia stood before them like a gaunt Tragic muse, fists pressed tight against her flat bosom.

"Thalia!" Miss Emily rapped sharply with her stick. Then her voice softened. "I'm sorry you had to hear of it like this. I meant to do it differently but—"

Miss Emily slumped in her chair. Finally she sighed. "Well, at last she knows."

17

While Judge Bo was consoling Miss Thalia, Don came in with Ronnie in tow and then stepped aside, letting Ronnie face his aunt and the others in his own way.

He bowed stiffly, almost ironically. "Cynthia, I'm sorry to intrude but I've come for my things. I won't disturb you again."

"Scrape it off and hang it up, Ronnie." Cynthia was being wearily cynical. "We all know you made the grade with the big shots, so don't rub it in."

Ronnie looked honestly bewildered. "Big shots? Made the— Oh!" He laughed softly. "You mean Bo? Is he a big shot? I just thought he was a pretty nice old egg."

"Why, thank you, Ronnie." Judge Bo spoke from behind Miss Thalia's quivering shoulder.

Ronnie peered into the gloom. "I wouldn't have said it quite that way if I'd known you were here, Judge. But Cynthia thinks this manufactured twilight is soooo correct." He stooped to peer, waving. "Hi, Miss Emily. Why, hello, Carol-Ann!"

He started toward her but Don put a quick stop to Ronnie's impetuous lunge across the room. "I have a couple of questions."

"Yes?" Ronnie turned back but not completely—enough to be courteous.

"How did you spend the evening? From seven on."

Ronnie raised his eyebrows. "You mean because Willie got his out there?" At Don's nod he shrugged politely. "Seven to quarter of eight—eating. A little after eight I offered to drive Bo over to Miss Marsten's but he said he preferred walking. This I do not believe was mere courtesy. After that dinner I know I needed a walk. However, I took my car and went—"

"To see Betty Lou." Cynthia made it sound like an assignation. For a moment Carol-Ann wondered if she was right and then was vexed at herself for even bothering to wonder. It was none of her business what Ronnie did.

Ronnie cocked his head toward Cynthia. "Why, my dear Aunt, I do believe you've become perceptive. That's precisely where I did go."

"Anybody see you?" Don cut across Cynthia's incipient screech of rage.

"Quite possibly. But you know my methods, Watson. The stealthy approach. I may have been spotted but I saw only Betty Lou—though I'm afraid you'd find it difficult getting her to testify to that." He grinned at Don.

"Collins wasn't there?" Don asked it with a familiarity that shocked Carol-Ann. Why, he even knew who should have been around a place like that!

"No, he'd gone home."

"And nobody saw you there?"

Ronnie looked at Don, then glanced around the room and back to him. He wasn't smiling now. "I believe you're serious. No. I suspect though that Tommy and that Ludovic kid were peeking through the window. I heard scufflings and whisperings."

"You better hope I can get something out of them. As it is, you're out one alibi."

Ronnie grinned ruefully and glanced at Cynthia. "That should make me popular around here."

"I don't know about that, but you're in excellent company." Don ticked them off on his fingers. "Luke Snedicker, Judge Bo, Mrs. Scudder."

"Cut it out!" Cynthia surged from her chair to face the two men. "And quit stalling, you." She aimed that directly at Don. "You know who done it, but you're covering up." She whirled, stabbing her finger at Carol-Ann. "Miss Puss Face. You know I seen her last night sneaking away from here."

Cynthia's justifiable anger didn't quite ring true. Carol-Ann could sense that. It was as if Cynthia had suddenly decided to create a diversion but what she was diverting from wasn't clear.

"I'm afraid I rile the lady," Ronnie apologized weightily to Don. "I'll just go pack my things." Ronnie faded neatly through the archway, leaving Cynthia with her finger still extended.

She lowered it slowly and slumped back in her chair, heels clicking petulantly. "He coulda done it," she said sullenly but without conviction. "Who believes that Betty Lou stuff anyway. And who is she? Jake tossed him out because of her." She flared up again briefly. "Only we all know it was Miss Baby Face." She tried to make it firm. "I tell you, I seen her leaving!"

Don gave Carol-Ann a brief, encouraging smile and began a patient explanation. "Miss Thalia has given Miss Foster an alibi for the murder of your husband, Mrs. Scudder, and I can give her one for the murder of Earps. We were heaving dinner together. In fact, those are the only three alibis I know are good. Mine, Miss Emily's and Miss Foster's . . . Oh—and your brother. He has an alibi. He's being held in—"

Cynthia subsided slowly into her chair, her sudden spurt of animosity dead, her face a controlled and rather beautiful blank.

"Or isn't he?" Don was already starting for the phone.

Luke Snedicker leaned forward, glaring at her. "I told you to let him stay there."

"Jails make him sick. You don't understand Andy. He's delicate. He needs—" Her voice broke to a whimper. "He told me to get a lawyer . . ."

"Who got him out of a nice, safe jail and put him on the spot. Maybe without an alibi." Luke sat back, narrowing his eyes at his late partner's wife. "Or maybe you like it like that?"

"Yeah! Maybe she does." Andy stood in the doorway, not exactly weaving but just unsteady enough to show he had been drinking. "So I'd get hanged."

"Andy!" Cynthia swirled out of her chair and flung herself at him. "Andy, Luke's just shooting off his mouth."

With the peculiar stateliness of the nearly drunk Andy drew himself up, brushing off her hands. "And hitting the target, baby? Or maybe coming close? So you wanta get ridda me, huh? Well, it didn't work, see. And jess for that I'm gonna tell this cop about you and that ugly little shrimp—" He made the mistake of taking his hands from the support of the door jamb to point to Luke and swayed into Cynthia's range.

"Shaddup!" Cynthia's claws raked down his face before he could get his hands up. "Shaddup!" Her fingers raked down again, but Don came up behind her and caught her elbows. She writhed and twisted and came up facing Don. "Don't believe that bum. I been covering for him all his life, and the devil with him from now on."

Andy clapped a hand to his cheek, pulled it slowly down, and stared at the smears of blood across his palm. It seemed to sober him momentarily.

"Sis!" It was sharp and incisive, snapping Cynthia's head around, so that she was glaring at him. He slumped against the frame of the archway, holding out his blood-streaked palm. "My little sister!"

Cynthia jerked once more in Don's grip and then stood very still, her eyes on Andy's face. She drew a deep, shuddering breath and let it out in a long sigh. "Andy, I'm sorry. I'm sorry!"

"Sure." Andy lurched upright, grinning. "All is forgiven. Everybody's pals again." He swept the room in a mockery of a bow.

"Touching!" Luke made it sound as tender and joyful as a drill on an aching tooth. "Such devotion. And I remember so well when it all happened." Luke smiled down at his manicure. "Right after Cynthia married a millionaire. You could scarcely wait for them to get back from their honeymoon, as I recall." Luke admired his other hand. "Long-lost brother returns. . . ."

"Why not?" Cynthia turned on Luke—and Carol-Ann could sense her control now. "I don't see Andy for years. I change my name for show business and he don't find me. But them pictures in all the papers—"

Luke wrote a headline in the air: "Showgirl Weds Millionaire." He dropped his hand as if the effort wearied him. "They were kind. Should have said 'Stripper A-Peels to Millionaire.'"

Cynthia shrugged with elaborate unconcern. "So tell everybody in town I was a peeler. I'm washed up here anyway."

"You were saying—" Don prompted Andy.

He looked blank. "Me?" He shrugged. "I forget what it was, so it couldn'ta been important."

"You were suggesting that your sister and Luke were—friends?" Don gave the question a barb. "Was Jake jealous?"

"Of him? Don't make me laugh." Nevertheless Andy laughed. "You think a dame like Cyn would pay attention to a dried-up squirt like him?" Andy slumped once more against the archway and looked around at Luke, squinting thoughtfully. "Not that Luke didn't try." The idea seemed to bloom, with the telling. "And Jake coulda caught him trying."

"Fantastic!" Luke's deliberate calm made the charge sound more fantastic than if he had shouted. "In fact, Jake knew such an eventuality was impossible."

Don glanced at Luke. "You know, it does sound as if you might have a motive."

"It was an accident. A premature explosion. In a mine. And it happened twenty years ago. I've had plenty of chances to kill Jake since. Better ones than this. On mining and construction jobs accidents can be made to happen."

"Another premature explosion?"

"That one was genuine. Jake almost lost an arm—and nearly died carrying me out." His thin face twisted into a rueful smile. "Ironically, it was that explosion that made us rich. It uncovered a lode."

"You figure that paid off the score?"

Luke hesitated, shook his head sadly. "It was—compensation. I could concentrate on making more money. I concentrated a little better than Jake, so I'm a little richer."

Don considered that. "You mean you didn't need to steal the forty-two thousand?"

So Don had gotten back to the theft of the money. Carol-Ann felt foolishly relieved. The theft of the money took the murder away from this little group of people she knew and put it on the shoulders of some anonymous thief.

Andy, however, seemed to take it personally. He lurched away from the arch and glared down at Luke. "You trying to say I needed money?"

"Shaddup!" Cynthia said it wearily, as if she no longer cared.

"Look who's sayin' shut up! My own sister! When this mug is trying to make a monkey outa me."

"You're doing all right on your own." Cynthia gave him small consolation. "I shoulda let you stay in jail. At least you'd have an alibi."

He whirled on her, tripped on the shag rug and almost fell. "I got one. I got not one but a lot of 'em." He held up one hand, fingers spread. He waggled one finger. "Jail—till your shyster got me out." Another. "The O Club." Another. "The deck." He looked up, peering through his fingers. "Hey, what'd I need an alibi for?" He glared suspiciously at Don through spread fingers. "Yeah. What d' I need an alibi for?" His voice went plaintive.

Cynthia told him, bluntly, brutally.

"Earps? Murdered?" Andy looked sick.

Don caught him as he started to sag and propped him against the frame of the archway, just as a young Trooper hurtled down the hall and into the room. He held out a newspaper-wrapped bundle to Don.

"We found these tucked back of the seat." He waved his free hand vaguely toward the road. "In Earps' car."

"Thanks." Don turned the support of Andy over to the Trooper while he unwrapped the bundle. He stared down into the nest of newspapers. "Well!" He reached down and picked up a pair of shoes.

Jake Scudder's shoes.

In sudden stillness Don thrust a hand down into the toe of each shoe and pulled out two wads of paper. He glanced at one, thrust it partly back, and continued to stare at the other, as if it made no sense, yet Carol-Ann knew it made a horrible kind of sense. She seemed to know what it was.

Don unfolded the stiff paper and turned it over twice before showing it to the room. It was a picture postcard, badly soiled, of the Azalea Gardens.

"Squiggles," was all he said.

With the shoes and that one silly, almost meaningless word he had tied the two murders together—and both of them to Miss Emily's bopping.

18

The discovery of Miss Emily's missing postcard tucked in the toe of Jake Scudder's shoe seemed to have stalled the investigation into Earps' murder— for that evening, at least.

Don had sent Andy staggering off to bed and the others had drifted away about their various concerns, apparently without police supervision. Carol-Ann suspected that wasn't quite the case, but from Miss Emily's upper guest bedroom she had seen no lurking figures. Did Don know, or suspect, who had done it?

There was no way of knowing, even the next morning. Things were quiet. Nothing seemed to be happening, though she knew that somewhere in official quarters the investigation went on relentlessly. For the moment, at least, interest in Earps and his death was incidental. The picture had broadened. The finding of Miss Emily's postcard had done that. It tied things together yet obscured them, too, in a way that left her feeling mentally bruised.

As Don patiently explained to her, the postcard must have been in Jake's den the night he was killed, and the murderer had stuffed it into Jake's outsized shoes to make them a temporary fit.

"But why was it in Jake's den?"

Don glared at her. Even Miss Emily glowered morosely, her massive head supported on hands clasped over the knob of her stick.

"Don't ask questions like that, child. You make my head ache worse than being clobbered." Miss Emily's head came up. "Clobbered! I got clobbered! For the postcard! Let me see it again."

The crumpling in the shoe and the subsequent police testing had not improved the legibility of the handwriting.

"I got it—and somebody didn't want me to have it. So I got clobbered. And the postcard snaffled. But why?" She glared defiantly at Carol-Ann. "I know I told you you couldn't ask questions like that but I can. I know they're coming and they don't bother me half as much."

Miss Emily glared at the card. "I must know a dozen people who write as badly as that."

"Well, it's no one on our list. Mrs. Scudder writes like a grade-school kid, but not that bad. Luke's fist is tight and cramped. Andy writes, oddly enough, like an educated man. Ronnie is the sloppy one, there. But again, not that bad. I even tested Jake's, but he's got a flat, thick scrawl but very legible. Judge Bo—"

"I know his handwriting. Looks like an educated spider got in the ink and walked across the page. And you can't read a word. Thalia's is the same way. And anyway, none of them have been in Charleston recently."

"Not that we can prove. Except for Ronnie."

"Ronnie?"

"He flew down on business for his uncle. But don't get excited. It was the day after the card was mailed and after Ted had left Charleston for Albemarle Sound. We got Ted's schedule from the Charleston gas man. Ronnie says he flew down and back the same day, and plane manifests say the same thing. Anyway, Ronnie's writing doesn't match. Neither does Ted's."

"Ted?" Miss Emily nodded. "Yes. You'd check his. He was in Charleston. He could have written that card."

"Except it was mailed after he left."

"But you wouldn't know that till after you'd checked." Miss Emily considered it again. "And now Ted's been murdered. You're sure it was murder?"

Don nodded glumly. "Bludgeoned with a brass belaying pin. Made to look like the boom had struck him, but that didn't fool the Coast Guard for long. Weapon found and identified, but no fingerprints. And very few on the boat. I understand he kept her ship-shape. What prints we did find were just about what you'd expect. And mostly old. His, yours—"

"Mine?" Miss Emily scowled and then nodded. "Yes."

"Eddie, the yacht club steward—some child's . . ."

"Ted was fond of children. He let them play aboard."

"Miss Thalia's, Judge Bo's, Phil Carsons'—he's a marine inspector—Ronnie's . . ."

"I didn't know Ronnie knew Ted. But then, I didn't know he knew Bo until last night. My intelligence department is slipping. I'll have to speak to Cassie. So Ronnie was aboard? Hmmm."

"He claims he was aboard up here, and that seems valid. At least that he made those particular prints up here. Carson's are superimposed in several places and he was the last one aboard before Ted sailed, and helped him cast off. Anyway, we've about given up on Ronnie as a suspect. He'd been cut out of Jake's will and knew it. If Jake had lived he might have put him back in. He usually did, Luke told us."

"Luke? Helped somebody?"

"Luke isn't so bad. He's scrupulously fair. Now Andy. . ." Don seemed to cheer up at the mere thought and then sighed. "But his prints aren't on the card or Ted's boat. He could have worn gloves, of course."

"Then Ted's murder is linked to Jake's—and Earps'?"

"Officially, no." Don sighed. "And even unofficially I can't think of a thing to connect Ted Marsten, slugged on a boat in Albemarle Sound, over a hundred miles away, with Jake Scudder, millionaire, stabbed in his own home, and a courthouse character stuck with an icepick in his car. Except this postcard."

"Ted and Jake were both robbed," Miss Emily pointed out. "Was Earps?"

"He didn't have anything to be robbed of—not that we know about."

"Nobody suspected Ted had nine thousand dollars—and I still can't believe it."

"He had it. The Bank of Virginia Beach handed it to him. In cash. Not nine, ten thousand. A thousand of it he spent. He settled a lot of bills before he left, bought supplies, gas, things like that."

"Where would Ted get ten thousand dollars? He'd sold off most of Judge Marsten's holdings years ago."

Don shook his head, turning toward the window. "We don't know. He deposited it in cash and drew it out in cash."

"Ted never did anything dishonest in his life," Miss Emily defended him.

"Most legitimate deals of that size are handled by check." Don stared out the window. "I've got to attend the reading of Jake's will in ten minutes." He leaned forward to peer. "Oh no! I don't believe it!"

Miss Emily erupted from her chair, beating Carol-Ann to the window. Suddenly she laughed. "Even in 3-D I wouldn't believe it."

Carol-Ann crowded in between them in time to see the smart new car drawn up in front of Miss Emily's and watch the dapper, slender figure in beige gabardine slacks, a dusty-green pullover sweater over a rich chocolate brown sports shirt clamber out and start up the walk. The figure seemed vaguely familiar. Then she recognized him. She stifled an impulse to giggle.

"I think he looks cute."

"Well, spring comes late—" Miss Emily heaved herself around and was at the door in time to open it before he rang. "Come in, Judge Bo."

Miss Emily caught his extended hand and tugged him into the room. "You don't look like you need a drink, but you make me feel like I do. Come in."

"Thank you, Emily I really can't stay. I've just been scouring the neighborhood looking for . . . Oh, there you are, Sergeant Corley."

"Howdy, Judge. That's a snappy outfit."

"You like it?" He sounded dubious but nevertheless preened as he turned half around and back for inspection. "Ronnie thought I ought to live up to my house. Go modern, you might say. He's even taught me to drive."

"That's fine." Don hesitated. "You were looking for me?"

Judge Bo blinked, looking regretful that his brief moment was waning. "Yes. Yes, I was. Er— You see, I've just come from talking to Thalia—Miss Marsten—and she persuaded me I should see you. Immediately." The Judge ended his speech abruptly, as if that was all he intended to say.

Don waited for him to go on, and when he didn't, rubbed his nose thoughtfully. "Something private, Judge?"

"Private?" Judge Bo seemed to remember there should have been more to his speech. "Oh, no. Distinctly not. I'm afraid it will be rather public. Perhaps unpleasantly so. That's the way those things go, isn't it?" He cocked his head and peered beadily up at Don.

Don glanced helplessly at Miss Emily, appealed mutely to Carol-Ann for guidance, then managed a shrug all on his own. "I don't know. Not necessarily. I mean—just what is it?"

"Oh yes! Certainly. I'm afraid I haven't made myself very clear, have I? You see, Tha—Miss Marsten suggested that I came to you privately there might be—less unpleasantness. Might, shall we say, close the investigation."

"Close the investigation?"

"Yes. That seemed to be Tha—Miss Marsten's idea. You see, I came to make a confession."

Miss Emily did not look like a person who could wilt but somehow she wilted, sagging into her chair, her wise old eyes suddenly very tired. "Not you, Judge Bo!"

He drew himself up stiffly. "Yes, I'm afraid it is I. In the beginning I didn't think of it as a crime. And in many ways, I still don't. Yet—"

Don exploded. "You don't think murder is a crime?"

"Murder?" Judge Bo looked baffled. "Murder? Oh, dear me. I haven't killed anyone. Well, not since the Spanish-American War, and I wasn't even sure then I hit him."

Miss Emily thumped her stick. "Then what the blazes are you confessing to?"

"Oh yes. To be sure. Well, it started as a rather harmless little deception. Well, taxes are rather high, you know, and Ted hasn't much—hadn't much, I should say. So when I gave him the money, I gave him cash." He smiled briefly at Don. "It can't be traced that way, you know. For taxes. You can save quite a bit in taxes on ten thousand dollars."

"What on earth did you give Ted ten thousand dollars for, Bo?"

"Commission. The sale of my house, you know."

"Ten thousand! That's an outrageous commission, Bo. You should never have paid it. I'm ashamed Ted asked so much."

Judge Bo looked meekly uncomfortable. "I know. But it was rather a delicate negotiation, Emily. And I simply couldn't talk to that man Scudder. He shouts. Quite a common person, really. Vulgar." He appealed to Don. "Does this have to be given er—ah—undue publicity? It isn't as if I profited by the transaction. And Ted is— gone."

"That's between you and Internal Revenue," Don offered, not too graciously. "If you haven't already made a false return."

"Oh, I haven't—"

"Just report it." Don turned away. "I have another appointment."

"So have I." Judge Bo delivered a hasty but thorough round of goodbyes and trotted after Don.

When the door had closed on them Carol-Ann felt as let down as Don had looked. "When Judge Bo began that rambling confession I really thought the case was ended." She sighed at Miss Emily. "Poor, confused little man."

Miss Emily snorted. "He's not poor since he sold Holly Hall and he's by no means as confused as you think. You may not have noticed, but Judge Bo just picked up a neat tax deduction on ten thousand dollars. There's nothing confused about that kind of thinking."

Carol-Ann tried to puzzle it out. "I don't get it."

Miss Emily sighed. "Oh, I don't doubt Thalia talked him into telling Don, but do you realize that now that the secret is out, Bo can write off that ten thousand as tax deduction, when he couldn't before. Ted would have had to pay the tax, but he's dead and the money's gone. So no one is hurt but Uncle." Miss Emily sighed again. "Why can't I think of things like that?"

19

While Jake's will was being read in the den, Carol-Ann decided to pick up some of her things she'd need if she were going to stay at Miss Emily's until Cynthia gave up the big house, as Carol-Ann was sure she would. Certainly the fantastic term of employment as social secretary was over and, even if it wasn't, Carol-Ann meant to terminate it. She and Miss Emily were just digging Carol-Ann's golf clubs out of the hall closet when the doors of the den burst open and Cynthia stormed out, her face livid and twisted with rage.

She turned back, screaming at someone in the den. "You did it, you stinker! You snooping—" A sob engulfed the rest of it, and her slim, elegant body was shaking. "He didn't hafta say it! I hate him! I hate him! I hate him! He didn't hafta say I wasn't married to him. Write it out in his will!"

It was violent, but Cynthia's rage wasn't nearly as great as her grief. That was genuine—so real it hurt to watch her. Her head rolled on her arm and her body shook. She turned around, holding her arm before her eyes and slumped against the wall, sobbing like a child unjustly spanked. "He didn't hafta do that to me—"

Luke Snedicker stepped through the door and stood beside her, hand half outstretched to comfort her. He thought better of it and reached into his pocket, producing a handkerchief. "Here, Cynthia—"

She groped for it and blew her nose. "Luke, I was good to him. I was straight. I—"

"He knew that, Cynthia."

She balled the handkerchief into a knot, pressing it against her forehead. "Then why—"

"He had to." Once more Luke reached in his pocket. Carol-Ann saw the slim white envelope as he handed it to Cynthia. "He left that with me for you. In case you didn't understand. Jake was a pretty swell guy."

Cynthia sniffled into the handkerchief, staring at the envelope. "Yeah, a pretty swell stinker! Writes it right out in his will—'the woman known as my wife'! Why'n don't he just say right out—"

"Cynthia!" Luke's voice was peremptory. "Read that letter!"

Cynthia gulped once, nodded and opened the letter with shaking fingers. "What can he say he ain't already said. And I was married to him, Luke. At least to me it was for real."

"It was to Jake, too. Read that letter." Abruptly Luke was gone.

Cynthia moved slowly across the hall, her fingers still fumbling with the envelope, as if she couldn't bring herself to look at the letter. She passed Carol-Ann and Miss Emily without seeing them and slumped ungracefully into a chair. She opened the single sheet of paper and scanned it hastily, her lips moving. Then she went back and read it slowly, until her eyes brimmed with tears and she turned to bury her face against the back of the chair, the hand with the letter dangling loosely.

Miss Emily moved very quietly and bent over her, touching her shoulder. "Can I help?" Cynthia shivered once, violently, and shook her head.

"Nobody can help, now. Jake's dead. Really dead." She swung around in the chair, all her studied movements forgotten. She rubbed the back of her wrist across her nose, like a small child. "It ain't seemed real till now—reading what he wrote and thought when he was alive." She held up the letter. "I wish I'da knowed he felt like that. But he wasn't much for talking love stuff, Jake wasn't."

"Do you want me to read this?"

Cynthia's face crumpled and she hid behind her hands. "I wish the whole world could read it! That's what a man thinks about the woman he loves—even a woman like me."

Miss Emily read softly, her harsh old voice gentled.

"Dearest Cyn: I don't know how to say I love you, so I just do things, like trying to give you everything you want and ought to have, but even that ain't enough. Not for you. Giving things is never enough. I tried to protect you, too, but sometimes you won't let me. So I know something bad is wrong. I figured out one thing, baby. We ain't married. That divorce you're supposed to have got ain't real, but I figure you know that and I figure you're paying plenty and was scared in the bargain. Or maybe there's something else I don't know and can't figure and I ain't been able to ask. So I had a couple of smart lawyers cook up that will. It don't say you ain't my wife and it don't say you are. It just identifies you. Just my Cynthia. That way, nobody can break the will or come up with legal tricks and take a cut. Or even put the bite on you any more. The money's all yours. Every penny I got. No strings. And it's yours as Cynthia, the woman known as my wife. So's the Tayloe house deed. That makes it legal and all yours, the lawyers say. So if somebody's trying to put the squeeze on you, baby, on account of us not being married, you're out of the bind. I hope I done what was best for you, baby. I love you.

Jake."

Miss Emily laid the letter on the table.

"I shoulda trusted him. I shoulda told him—" Cynthia pounded her knees with her fists. "But I was scared I'd lose him. And I woulda. My first husband—" She smiled ruefully up at Miss Emily. "I guess I oughta say my real husband—he'da fixed that. Like he did that phony divorce he said we had. He wouldn'ta never given me a real one, not after I was married to Jake. And Jake was in a spot then—with all them government contracts—where he couldn't have a scandal."

"So you just shut up and paid? To protect Jake." Miss Emily scowled down at Cynthia. "I think you were an idiot. But somehow, it's the kind of idiocy I like. And when you get your face together, we'll get out of this house for a while. Go over to my place for tea." Miss Emily thought that over ferociously. "With brandy."

"Me? Have tea with you?" Cynthia's face crumpled and she reached out blindly. Miss Emily's stout, capable arms cradled her, rocking her gently. Cynthia sniffled happily. "Jake woulda liked that. Me having tea with you." She pushed herself away from Miss Emily's ample bosom and smiled pleadingly. "Could I pour?"

Miss Emily grinned. "Sure. If you tuck your pinky under."

Cynthia's artificial beauty was irradiated, for once, with pure, impish pleasure, and it made her a truly lovely woman.

After Cynthia had gone to put her face together, Miss Emily grinned at Carol-Ann. Then, listening intently to some distant sound, the grin ceased. "Come on. We gotta get him—" And Miss Emily lunged recklessly for the hall, and out the side door.

It is difficult to drive a flamboyantly modern car in broad daylight and appear furtive, but Andy had achieved it. Even with his head craned around to watch his reverse steering, he looked hunched and sly and menacing. Or am I just reading that into him? Carol-Ann started to call out, and then decided to save her breath.

Ahead of her Miss Emily let out a screech that snapped Andy's head around. Miss Emily waved her stick. "Wait for me."

Andy took one look at the massive figure bearing down on him—and stepped on the gas. The tomato-bisque convertible roared and surged backwards down the drive, headed for the gap between the oleanders, just as a police car rolled in. There was a splintering crash, a grinding of metal, the thin, high tinkle of breaking glass.

Without looking back even to survey the damage, Andy crouched over the wheel of the convertible and almost seemed to lift it forward in a roaring surge. The convertible lunged, and then, as Carol-Ann watched, horror-stricken, Andy swerved it deliberately toward Miss Emily, roaring across the yard at her.

Carol-Ann couldn't swear afterward that it happened. It may have been an illusion. She thought she saw Miss Emily lift her stick like a javelin, heavy silver knob first, and let go. A walking stick, even Miss Emily's outsized job, is a feeble weapon with which to attack a charging automobile. But to the man inside the car the stick, hurtling straight and true at the windshield, must have looked like an oncoming comet. Andy ducked and swerved. The car hurtled past Miss Emily, missing her by an inch. And as it went by she used the last of her hurling momentum to slam her fist against Andy's jaw.

The car spurted on. The front wheel caught in a low, tough shrub. The car slewed, skidded forward, the two left wheels trying frantically to climb a thick and stubborn privet hedge. The hedge gave, bent and then sprang back as the convertible rolled over on its side, wheels churning futilely. Andy's limp figure sprawled out across the grass.

Miss Emily was still blowing on her knuckles as she ambled up and looked down at him. Don came at a run, revolver in his hand. He stared down at the sprawled figure. Almost fearfully he glanced at Miss Emily. "What did you do to him?" He looked at the shambles. "Aside from mayhem?"

Miss Emily sighed. "I think he misunderstood me. I was just asking for a lift in to town when he—"

"I hope you never decide to thumb a ride with me." Don holstered his gun and nudged Andy with his toe. "Get up. You're not hurt." He glared at Miss Emily. "Somebody owes the state for a new police cruiser." He nudged Andy again. "I said get up."

"He won't. He's sitting on a lot of money he doesn't want you to see. Or maybe he's just trying to hatch more."

Carol-Ann peered around Don's broad back at Andy and saw the crisp green of bills protruding from under the fallen man.

At that moment Ronnie strolled up and took in the wreckage. He whistled softly, shaking his head. He glanced at Miss Emily, Don, and finally Carol-Ann.

Andy glared up at them, huddling around the bills. He shivered slightly as Don nudged him once more.

"What money is that?" Don reached down and snagged a bill, studying it.

"I think you'll find it is the forty-two thousand missing from Jake's den." Miss Emily took the crisp bill from Don, turned it over, then handed it back. "A new fifty. Ted had new fifties."

Don nodded. "Right. And the serial number checks. Lord knows I've read enough reports to remember them."

"Then he killed Ted?"

"I'll enjoy asking him." Don reached down for a fistful of padded shoulder and hauled Andy to his feet, money spilling off him as a burst suitcase dribbled more bills on to the lawn. Andy looked down at them, closed his eyes and swayed weakly.

Cynthia came running across the lawn, her eyes wide and staring as she saw the scattered money. Then they narrowed to deadly menace as they raked Andy's face. "I'm glad they got you. I'm glad it was Miss Emily got you. Because if it had been me, I'da killed you." Her heel ground viciously into the turf. "And you're not worth it."

Miss Emily took Cynthia's arm. Tucking it under one of hers, she turned her away. "Andy isn't your brother, is he?"

"No."

"Your first husband?"

"Yes— Oh, Miss Emily—" And once more cool, impervious Cynthia wept in Miss Emily's arms. Miss Emily let her cry it out, patting her shoulder. Finally she thrust one hand under her chin. "Straighten up. I bet you never let Jake see you cry."

"He'da laughed at me. Or batted me one."

"Maybe not. You should have tried it."

Cynthia nodded. "Maybe I shoulda." She smiled uncertainly. "Anyway, we had a lot of laughs together—so maybe I didn't need to cry."

"I think that calls for that tea." Miss Emily started across the lawn. "Right now."

Cynthia slowed to a halt and looked at Miss Emily, smiling. "You know, maybe I'm learning what it takes to be a lady."

Miss Emily jerked her along. "Better than that. You've known all along how to be a woman."

20

The sour smell of the jail even seeped through into Don's office, making Carol-Ann feel sickish. Or maybe she was just sick of looking at Andy, smirking back in the office chair, blithely sure of himself. He sighed mockingly at Don's question.

"I tole you how it happened. Maybe fifty times."

"Try for fifty-one. The ladies would like to hear it."

Carol-Ann felt the sliminess in Andy's eyes as they slid over her, flicked contemptuously past Miss Emily and raked over Cynthia huddled on a hard bench across the room. "Okay." He gave a martyred shrug. "I figured the front door would be bolted, so I come around to the side and there was a light on in the den. I peeked in and Jake looked like he was snoozing, so I figured it was safe—so I figured I'd go in that way. Only he wasn't snoozing. He was dead. Right?"

"This is your version."

"He was dead, all right. It's sorta up to you to prove he wasn't, anyhow." Andy dismissed this technicality with another shrug. "So I picked up the dough, figuring to keep it safe. From cops. I didn't want to see another Greenlease split." Andy winced as Don started from his chair, but he kept talking. "I unlocked the den and went—"

"Mrs. Scudder was in the living room and didn't see anybody come out."

"I didn't go to the front hall. I went to the back stairs so I could get to a telephone and call the cops. Trying to be helpful, see. Only just after that you come busting in and I didn't need to call copper."

"You didn't tell this story then."

"I'm telling it now."

Don sighed. "Okay. So you were going to call the police. Why didn't you use the phone in the den?"

"Why, copper, ain't you ever been told not to mess up evidence? I didn't want to louse up any fingerprints." Andy smirked virtuously. "So, copper, you got nothing on me."

"We've got fifty-one thousand dollars on you." Don touched the money stacked on his desk. "Forty-two thousand of that belonged to Jake Scudder."

"Come off it. That money didn't belong to Jake. It was Cynthia's dough. Jake deeded her the house—and when he sold it, the dough belonged to her. I just took charge of it." He settled back in the chair, hands behind his head. "And since it was Sis's dough, ask her if she's gonna prosecute."

"Mrs. Scudder isn't your sister. She's told us the story. You faked a divorce, waited around until she married again, and then moved in on her. That's blackmail."

Andy shrugged. "Is she gonna prosecute on that?" He glanced across at Cynthia, grinning crookedly. "How about it?"

Cynthia stirred slowly and sat up. Her eyes went first to Miss Emily, then to Carol-Ann with a warmth that was surprising. "I don't know. Miss Emily told me my story'd get me a lot of sympathy in this town—which I didn't figure it had any. But now that I know that it has," she crinkled her nose at Carol-Ann, "I kinda like it. So I just might prosecute—for blackmail."

Andy stiffened, a little of his smug assurance drying up. "Now, look—"

"About stealing the money, I don't care. That wasn't my dough. It's Franky Lund's."

"Lund's?" Andy laughed, but not too bravely. "How does that figure?"

Cynthia waved her hand airily. "Oh, Jake never gave him the deed. Just a receipt—and that ain't much good with Jake dead." She was doing it with all the off-hand glibness Miss Emily had rehearsed her for. "And anyhow, since the publicity, Franky don't want the house. But he does want his dough. All of it. The other eighteen thousand, too."

Andy squealed shrilly. "That wasn't dough! That was I.O.U.s. They were for—"

"You want to tell the cops all about it? With Franky waiting outside?" Cynthia waved a hand delicately toward the frosted panel of the door. She peered at Miss Emily for approval and got it.

Andy's jauntiness deserted him. He sank back, wetting his lips. "It was just some money I owed him."

Don ignored the man and glanced at Cynthia. "Then this goes back to Lund?" He swept three stacks of bills toward an open drawer, pausing for her reply.

Cynthia looked at Miss Emily for her cue and then nodded. "Sure. It's his."

Andy watched the money disappearing into the open maw of the desk. Suddenly he lurched forward. "Hey!" He swiveled toward Cynthia. "How'm I gonna live?"

Cynthia shrugged. "With three murder raps hanging over you and eighteen grand of Franky's dough still owed, I figure the question is . . . how're you gonna die? But I'm not curious. I can wait." She waved airily and sat back as if she were prepared to wait it out right there.

It was a vicious game of cat and mouse, but one Carol-Ann felt Cynthia had bought the right to play, bought with years of torment at Andy's ruthless, greedy hands.

All of Andy's false youthfulness deserted him, leaving his face old and sick. He moved his head slowly, leaving his eyes on Cynthia until the last moment, as if he were afraid she might leap at him. Then his eyes jerked to Miss Emily—to Carol-Ann—to Don. "I didn't kill nobody." It was scarcely more than a whisper.

Don tapped the two remaining bundles of bills. "Ted had these the day he left Charleston. We've got three witnesses, prominent business men. The money was missing when he was found dead in Albemarle Sound. It turned up in your suitcase." It was a deadly array of facts that beat Andy back into his chair, where he sat gnawing his lip. He swallowed gulpily and then color surged into his sallow face.

He leaned forward eagerly. "I got it. I got it." He stabbed a finger at Don. "I got an alibi. And you give it to me. Yeah!" He drew a deep, shuddering breath. "I was in jail. Three days. Drunken driving. I was supposed to drive Cynthia to that stinkin' flower show and look at zinnias. Only I got looped." He whirled to appeal to Cynthia. "You remember. Jake would let you bail me . . ." His voice petered out under the blank look Cynthia returned. He sneered at her. "Naw, you wouldn't want to remember." He swung back to Don. "But it's in the records. It's right there." His finger quivered at a wooden card file on the desk. "Just look in there. Look! Go ahead!"

Don toyed with the lid of the box and Miss Emily sat forward for the first time, leaning heavily on her stick. "Wouldn't it be awkward, Don, if those records were lost?"

Don slapped the wooden box hard. "Come to think of it, Corporal Stagg has been a little careless lately. I must speak to him about that. Misplacing records." He clucked dolefully.

The spurt of eagerness died out of Andy's eyes, leaving them black, hopeless. His mouth opened and closed, opened and hung there, shuddering. He gulped his mouth shut. "You're framing me!"

"Now, Andy, about this nine thousand dollars."

Andy made an effort to straighten up and look decisive but it didn't work. "It was just like that. In two bundles. On top of the rest. I thought it was part of what Lund had paid Jake. How could I tell different? Dough's dough."

"Uhn-huhn." Don nodded gravely. "You said that before. Now let's have the real story." His hand tapped the file case absently. "Where'd this money come from?"

"I swear to—" Andy wiped the rest of it away with an unsteady hand. He pulled both hands to his knees and tried for control. "Jake had a real estate deal on. A big one. I heard them talking about it—Marsten was handling it for him."

"We know about that."

Andy looked momentarily surprised, then shrugged. "So Ronnie fixed the pay-off. In cash. That was the way Marsten wanted it."

"That isn't the way we heard the story."

Carol-Ann tried to think back to exactly what Judge Bo had said. She couldn't remember, but she didn't think he'd said he actually handed the money to Ted Marsten. Ronnie could have done it.

"Maybe they didn't handle it just that way." Andy pretended he couldn't care less. "But that's what they planned."

"So Ronnie knew Marsten would have ten thousand dollars."

Andy snatched at that. "Yeah! Yeah, Ronnie knew. Sure. He knew Marsten had the dough."

Don nodded pleasantly. "And so did you."

Andy's bright, brief bubble of hope exploded. He nodded sullenly. "Yeah, I knew. But he tucked it right in the bank—"

"So you were watching him?"

Andy tried to think his way out of that one. He spoke slowly. "Just keeping an eye on him. Y'see, I had a little deal I figured Marsten might go for. But before I could talk to him, he took off in that boat of his. I didn't even know he'd taken the dough outa the bank."

"Even though you were keeping an eye on him?" Don sounded skeptical.

Andy seemed to resent the impugnment of his ability more than the slur on his character. "Aw, he had a blazing scrap with that skinny sister of his and stormed outa the house. And blooey! He was gone. How'd I know he'd grab the dough and run? Every time him and that female scarecrow had a fuss he'd light out for that boat of his. I ast her a coupla times where he'd gone but she didn't know. Just said she never went near the boat."

Don went on. "So Marsten took off for Charleston, with ten thousand dollars. When did you follow him?"

"I didn't follow him."

"Why was Earps hanging around Jake's house."

"I don't know. . . ." Andy had an inspiration. He twitched with eagerness to tell it. "Willie saw the deed to Holly Hall, where Jake says, just like in the will . . ." Andy brooded over this injustice a moment, sighed, and went on. "You know, where he says 'the woman known as my wife'—and Willie smelled a rat. He was good at things like that. He tried to pump me." Andy shrugged.

"Naturally you didn't satisfy his curiosity. That would have spoiled your game."

"Who'd tell Willie the time of day? He'd try to make a buck out of it, if you did." Andy raked the sweat from his jaw. "I figure Willie sneaked around to try something. Maybe put the bite on Jake about that 'woman known as my wife'—only while he was snooping, he seen something."

"Yes." Don nodded. "That's how we figure it. And we think what he saw was you—committing murder."

Andy's animation died and he shook his head wearily, almost as if he himself weren't convinced. "Not me."

"Why did you wear Jake's shoes over to Miss Thalia's?"

"I didn't."

"Why did you steal the postcard from Miss Emily?" Why? . . . Why? . . . The questions came fast and faster until Andy was jerking his head from side to side as if he could physically dodge them. But he could only offer flat denials. They got no more out of him that night. They never got any more out of him. At eleven they stuck him in a cell.

The turnkey heard the shot just after midnight and ran in to him. Andy was already dead.

The State Police Commissioner threatened to break eight men in his efforts to find where Andy had gotten the gun, an old thirty-two of common make.

21

The little man who backed out of the front door ahead of Cynthia's fury was so flamboyantly correct in his tailoring that he didn't look nearly as small as he actually was. Miss Emily and Carol-Ann had to let him step backwards between them before they realized he was almost a midget. The deception was mostly in the coat, elegantly cut, with a magnificent drape, but verging on the mustard, with rather an alarming green plaid overlaying it. His trousers were correctly cut and faintly mauve, with overwide lavender stripes running down them, creating the odd optical illusion of a small man wearing stilts. Even in its creamy perfection, his Panama was outsize, with a crown slightly too high and a broad, sharply rolled brim. He was magnificent and magnificently aware of it, even in retreat. "But my dear lady—"

"I'm not a lady. I never was a lady. Not even an Act of Congress can make me a lady. Hello, Miss Emily . . . Carol-Ann. Now scram, creep." Cynthia was obviously enjoying herself now that she was no longer under the strain of being elegant. Even her hair was loosened from its tortured, metallic curls and fell softly around her face. She swept back a lock with one hand and grinned at Miss Emily, winked at Carol-Ann. "This kind of character I can handle. Beat it, you . . ." The shoulder tap she gave him didn't look strong but it spun the little man around and sent him teetering toward the stairs.

He caught his balance and swung back to her. "There has been a mistake somewhere."

"And you're it. Now blow, schmoe. Come in, Miss Emily, Carol-Ann. What a character!"

The little man seemed to snatch cards out of the air— outsized cards but beautifully engraved, as Carol-Ann saw when he thrust one into her hand. She stared at it in amazement.

Carnivals	Midways	Shows
Rides	*Colonel I. M. Small*	Games
	Impressario	
Carousels	Kiddie Rides	Fun Houses

He pressed one into Miss Emily's hand. "Colonel Small at your service. Carnival, shows and midways. Rides, games and . . ."

Miss Emily was gazing at the card with what Carol-Ann was appalled to notice was just a trace of wistfulness. Then she got a firmer grip on herself, and handed it back. "Sorry. I already own a carnival." She sighed. "Or I might as well. Tex Billings will never pay the mortgage."

"Tex!" The little man boomed it exuberantly in a surprisingly loud voice. "Good old Tex. Great fellow, Tex. So you know Tex, do you?" The little man edged himself back into the group, much to Cynthia's consternation. Miss Emily caught it and turned to the little man who reached up to grasp her hand, booming again. "Well, well. So you know Tex."

"Never heard of him." And Miss Emily sailed through the door, somehow collecting Carol-Ann and Cynthia in her wake and closing the door behind her in the bewildered face of the little man. She looked back through the glass and made a face at him. Alarmed, the little man backed off, turned and scurried away. She straightened and looked at Cynthia. "Did you get him with ten cents and six box tops?"

Cynthia laughed. Not her tinkling, artificial laughter Carol-Ann had been accustomed to hearing, but real, genuine laughter. "Miss Emily, you'll be the death of me—" Slowly she sobered and shook her head.

"I'm glad you didn't come wearing black gloves and carrying a card." She swept out a hand to indicate the pile of cards on a silver salver. "Half the town was here, now that Andy has cleared things up by committing suicide. They said they came to honor him. Honor Jake! And they wouldn't speak to him when he was alive." Her lovely mouth softened, trembled. "He was a great guy, Miss Emily."

"And he could be as mean as a snake and crooked as a ram's horn—"

Cynthia gasped, her face whitening, her eyes going hard. "Now, look here! Even from you—"

"But he was still a great guy, Cynthia. Just don't idolize him. A dead idol is awful hard to live with. Look at Thalia. The old Judge was about as vain, arrogant and stupid an old coot as they come, but she's wrecked her life trying to live with an idol of him. She's puffed him up into a little tin god. Don't do that to yourself—or to Jake. He was too real a guy." Miss Emily errumphed violently. "Now find me a chair I can sit in comfortably."

Cynthia found them chairs and slumped back in hers with unstudied casualness. "Thanks for the spiel. I won't make that blooper again. Or not often, anyway. All I gotta do is remember some of the bullhead stunts Jake pulled. Like fighting with Ronnie. They shoulda been pals. I asked him to come home but he likes it at Judge Bo's. And it gives him more time for Betty Lou. Now that was stupid of Jake, that Betty Lou argument. Or fighting with Luke.

Luke's smart. Smarter than Jake. He shoulda listened to him and then we wouldn'ta that character out front." She looked at the card in her hand. "Colonel I. M. Small!" She tore the card in two, dropped the pieces in an ashtray. "What a jerk!"

"Was Jake planning to buy a carnival? That isn't so stupid. They make money." Miss Emily brooded on that for a moment. "All except mine."

"You really own a carnival?" Cynthia looked at her wide-eyed, as if she expected her to break out in spangles.

"When you get to be as rich as I am—which most likely you are—you'll find you turn up owning a lot of queer things."

"Yeah. Jake woke up one day owning a battleship. It was second-hand, though." Cynthia scowled over that. "Maybe I still own it. I don't remember him selling it. What'dya do with a second-hand battleship?"

Miss Emily sighed. "You might have some fun owning a carnival."

"Not that one. I carry a ten-foot pole specially not to touch it with. That's the one cost me the Madam Chairman."

"You mean somebody found out you were once in it?" Miss Emily lifted stout arms and waggled them. "Ta-da-boom, boom, boom."

Cynthia giggled. "Nope. I never did a tent show. It wasn't that. Jake was smart in lots of ways but he just couldn't figure you folks. And it wasn't a carnival. A sort of amusement park. Rides, whirls, leap-the-dips, fun house, roller coaster, Ferris wheel."

"Like Coney Island?" Miss Emily's eyes lit happily. Then her enthusiasm dulled. "It would never do for Virginia Beach. Brings in a cheap element and lowers our lordly prestige. It would also lower our lordly real estate values."

"That's what Miss Marsten said. Only louder. And more of it. I don't think Jake really meant to bring it in. Just sorta let her get the idea that he might—if I didn't get made Madam Chairman. Only she didn't fall for it. Just pretended to until . . . . well, she bounced me off that committee so hard I still feel pain. Yow!"

Miss Emily clucked. "I'm surprised at Jake. He should have realized Thalia knew he could never put up an amusement park here. She gulled him. There isn't enough land left in town to build a dog house for a chihuahua, let alone an amusement park."

"Oh, Jake had that worked out with Ted Marsten. That's why he gave him the ten grand. For a binder."

"Well, if anybody knew where land was available, it would be Ted." Miss Emily sat back thoughtfully, her eyes going over Carol-Ann's head. Very slowly she smiled. "Well, if Judge Bo isn't a ring-tailed lallapalooza!" Miss Emily shook her head. "But who'da thought Bo was that smart? And I've been thinking that was the deal Andy was talking about."

"You mean Holly Hall?" Cynthia hesitated and then plunged on. "Look, Miss Emily, this town don't like me much, and it's mutual. Except for a few folks like you that's for real. But Holly Hall—well, you don't see me living in that museum, do you?"

Miss Emily surveyed Cynthia's modern perfection and shook her head. "Frankly, I never understood why you wanted to."

"Oh, in them days I was gonna be a great lady. Nuts! I wanta get rid of it."

Miss Emily shook her head. "Hard to sell, a big place like that. Except to somebody like Franky Lund."

"Uh-uh. Not Franky. A house like that, it's historic. A punk like Franky hadn't oughta have it for a night club and gambling joint. That's what Jake and me had a scrap about, the night he died. That and the amusement park. He wanted to go ahead and build it but . . . well, it's all right as a gag . . . but you can't do that to a whole town. But Jake was sore. Real sore at what happened to me. So— Anyway, that's over with." She brushed it aside with a swipe of her hand. "But I still got the house. And I was thinking—well—I'd like to . . . I mean, you've been so swell and there are real folks around here. So I'd like to give Holly Hall to the town."

Miss Emily considered it gravely and shook her head. "It wouldn't work." She watched Cynthia's mouth droop dejectedly.

"Yeah. I guess I should plug the holes in my head."

"The town couldn't afford to keep it up. A gift like that would scare 'em to death. But you could present it to the State. As a museum."

"Me?" Cynthia gulped uneasily. "Me give something to the State of Virginia?" Her eyes searched Miss Emily's face, pathetically suspicious of a gag. She appealed to Carol-Ann. "She kidding me?"

Carol-Ann put out a hand impulsively, covering one of Cynthia's. "Why should she? You made a hit with the Governor. You could just drop him a note, suggesting it."

"Me? Write to the Governor? Just like that—" She snapped her fingers. "I drop the Governor a note." She giggled. "Oh, gosh, you're a couple of wonderful people. You made it sound like I really could. Me, I'd feel like a kid writing to Santa Claus."

"You should feel like Santa Claus writing to the kid. You're the one giving things this time." Miss Emily started to prepare to rise. "And when you write, remember, it's the Commonwealth of Virginia, not the State. We're very proud of that 'Commonwealth'—not that I know why.

"And if there's any way we can help—with the funeral . . ." Miss Emily lunged erect.

"Gee, thanks. Luke has made all the arrangements. We're going to take him home." She walked with them to the door. "There is something, though. About Andy. I'm kinda in a spot there. I want to do the right thing. Nothing fancy. Just the right thing. But it's kinda hard to figure, when the cops have it settled he killed—" She broke off, her mouth trembling. "I just want to do what's right."

Miss Emily laid a comforting hand on her arm. "I'll talk to Don, and we can settle things when you drop over tomorrow."

Miss Emily thumped away, down the walk and across the street, lunging with a speed that Carol-Ann had to trot to match. "Fools! They're all fools. Don most of all if he thinks Andy's death settled this case. A complete fool."

"I'm not that much of one." Carol-Ann felt Don's arm slide under hers, and she was absurdly happy, until she realized what their two statements meant. Neither the police nor Miss Emily were at all sure the case was settled. Don shook his head at them both. "I can't just close a case because of a convenient suicide. A very convenient suicide."

"I wondered." Miss Emily didn't even break her halfback technique of crossing streets. "Oh, you may be a fool when you're around redheads, but I didn't think you'd be idiot enough to let a murder suspect take a gun into his cell. Or hand him one, either, after he got there. Nobody did."

Don's stride broke and then he caught up again. "Nobody did. That sounded profound. What's it mean. The gun was in his cell. Andy is dead. Bullet matches gun."

Miss Emily charged through her own front door, pivoted and flung herself into her favorite chair. "If Andy had gotten a gun in his hands, he'd have tried to shoot or bluff his way out. He didn't. Ergo he didn't have a gun."

"I don't get it." Don held a chair absently for Carol-Ann. "We found the gun in his cell." He grinned. "Ergo—he had it. Somebody slipped it to him. He commits suicide. Not . . ." Don let go of the chair to hold up a finger . . . "because he's a murderer. But because he's on seventeen different kinds of spots. We know he couldn't have killed Ted—and probably not Earps. But somebody gave him a gun. I want that somebody."

"Come here." Miss Emily whispered with much conspiratorial fervor that Don almost jerked the chair from under Carol-Ann in his haste to get to her. He leaned over Miss Emily. "You're in the cell. I'm at the window." She dug a stubby, ringed finger sharply in his ribs. "And this is a gun!"

Don stared down at the finger against his chest.

"Bang! You're dead."

Miss Emily tossed the imaginary gun on the floor.

They all looked at the spot on the floor where the weapon should be, and something like horror clamped down on Carol-Ann. Don swore softly, poked out a toe at the imaginary gun.

"Murder! Now I really want that somebody!"

22

The murders had seemed so neatly wrapped and put on the shelf with Andy's "suicide." Then, just because Miss Emily said "Bang! You're dead," everything started over again. At least for Carol-Ann.

It has been almost a week now since Jake's funeral and the quiet burial of Andy, and everybody else had gone back to normal, healthy, sunshiny lives along the beach and at the clubs. But not Carol-Ann. Not me. I still cringe at dropping pine cones and shy at forsythia bushes that loom at night. Don isn't around enough, and even then he's glum and irritable and . . . If he doesn't look out, I may not marry him. Why, I might not even propose to him, and then he'll never know what he's missed.

In this way Carol-Ann had talked herself back into nearly normal good humor and could go back to reading.

Carol-Ann didn't get back to her mystery though, because just as she picked it up, she heard a stealthy movement outside the summerhouse, between her and Miss Emily's big, rambling old house. And she could see a tiny patch of red that moved and stopped and moved in a stalking approach toward Miss Emily's front porch.

Miss Emily stumped out on her porch, raised one hand and peered under it, Indian fashion, as if she were trying to make out the perfectly obvious summerhouse.

"Bang!"

Carol-Ann saw Miss Emily jerk backwards and stagger. She caught at the rail with both hands and rocked violently.

"Bang! You're dead!" a small, strident voice screamed triumphantly from behind a wilting hydrangea.

The little figure held at steady bead what seemed to be an outsized six-shooter in such a small fist. One green eye squinted down the barrel and into Miss Emily's eye, which she promptly closed.

"One move and you're dead," announced a surprisingly large voice, made larger and shriller by excitement.

"I'm already dead," Miss Emily countered in her best hollow "dead" voice, collapsing alarmingly deeper into the wicker chair.

A small smile twinkled at the corners of a wide mouth and big green eyes lit mischievously. "Well, I figgered with you dead, you wouldn't need all those cookies Cassie made this morning." The daring suggestion died in another giggle.

"Well," said Miss Emily, her "dead" voice beginning to show the strain, "there's nothing to prevent you now."

Entering Miss Emily's big, cool old house, the little girl turned back and grinned, said, "You're not dead any more," and ran inside.

Carol-Ann laid down her book and hurried across the lawn. She caught up with Miss Emily in the big, cool living room and wondered briefly why she'd ever sought coolness outside. "Isn't that Dawn?" She nodded at the tiny red rump disappearing around the edge of the kitchen door. "I thought Commander Mathieson had been transferred."

The rump re-appeared and, some twenty inches above it, a head. The torso, by some elasticity of youth, had gone on around the door jamb. "My daddy is a Lieutenant Commander and he says it isn't fair to make out like he's a full commander. But Mildred does. That used to be my mommy, only I'm to call her Mildred now that I'm developing. Daddy wasn't transferred. He got sea duty and Mildred went down to Charleston so he couldn't meet any blondes if the fleet put in there, only it didn't, so we're back." Having fired this burst of information, the head disappeared, taking the rump along.

"Poor kid! She knows too much, and not enough to keep quiet about it. That Mathieson woman!" Carol-Ann stamped her foot. "If I had a cute kid like that, I would spend a little time with it, and not chase Don all over the map."

And then she plunged into the melee of the kitchen. Dawn had gotten as far as the back door when she turned. "Thank you, Miss Emily for the cookies. Now I have to go and help Judge Bo watch his ice-maker. I promised." She crinkled up her face at Miss Emily. "But you play a simply super game of Corpse and Robbers!" And she was gone.

Miss Emily sighed. "Corpse and Robbers! I should be able to play it. I've been practicing for a week. With real corpses. Cassie, do you still have strength enough to whip up a light snack?"

Carol-Ann wandered into the living room, leaving them happily planning a snack that sounded like preparations for a Confederate encampment.

A woman stood at the front door, elegantly silhouetted against the sunlit street, her hand raised to the knocker. Carol-Ann called out to her, "Come in."

The woman swept in. "Hello. Oh, you're Carol-Ann. I'm Mildred Mathieson, Commander Mathieson's wife. We're just back in town and I have a terrifically important bridge date and I simply can't find Dawn. That's my little girl. Dawn Wakiki." The voice went on in one swift monotone until Miss Emily thudded into the room. Miss Emily was more adroit and vigorous than Carol-Ann. Somehow she was maneuvering the still chattering woman toward the door, her stick working not unlike a shepherd's crook to keep the flighty women on the move.

At the little console table by the door, however, Mrs. Mathieson came to a shrill, squealing halt, like a car setting its brakes. Miss Emily almost collided with her as she reached out to grab the plastic-coated post card.

"My card! How simply divine! You've framed it! In plastic! How original! My dear Miss Emily, I'm so flattered! Imagine framing my poor little card." She caught it up, snuggling it close and rocking it like a child with a doll. "I'm so thrilled. You'll never know—"

Miss Emily braced herself, looming over the smaller woman. She glowered so ferociously that the commander's wife for once ran out of words. "You wrote that?" Miss Emily poked her and the card violently.

Mildred Mathieson drew back in alarm, taking a second cautious peek at the card. "Of course I did. I can read my own writing, I suppose."

"Nobody else can." Miss Emily snatched the card from her and held it up as if she were conducting an eye examination. "What's it say?"

"Well, really." The woman turned in tremulous appeal to Carol-Ann, who gave her no help, for she was concentrating on the scrawled writing. The woman flounced petulantly. "It's perfectly plain—"

"Then read it!" Miss Emily was not standing on courtesy.

The woman drew back her head, stared at Miss Emily, and then bent to peer at the card. "Why, it's plain as day. It says . . ." She bent nearer. "The light's bad here." She took the card from Miss Emily, her movements tentative and uncertain, as if she expected it to be snatched back. She turned her back to the light and peered at the card.

She smiled vaguely at them across the card and licked her lips. "It says, 'Dear Miss Emily:' Then it says, 'When you get to Charleston, look us up.' I do say that frequently. But, of course, you never expect people to—"

"Don't guess. Read."

Mrs. Mathieson looked as if she'd like to rebel as she bent over the card. "No, I think it's a 'Who.' Yes. The next word is 'do' and there's a 'think' right along there." Her finger stabbed at the card. Suddenly she beamed at them. "I know now. See! There's a 'Dawn' on the third line. Why, of course I can read it. It says, 'Who do you think Dawn saw here today?' There!" She handed back the card with a flourish. "It wasn't hard at all."

Miss Emily accepted the card, her eyes on the woman's flushed, triumphant face. "Well?"

Mrs. Mathieson fluttered her hands. "Well—what?"

"Who—I mean—whom did she see?"

"Oh," Mrs. Mathieson trilled gayly, "I never answer my own questions. It's silly, isn't it, asking questions and then answering them yourself. Anyway, it's so much more fun to guess, don't you think?"

"Not this time. Whom did Dawn see?"

Mildred Mathieson opened her hands gracefully. She had once been told that they were like petals unfolding and had never forgotten it. "How should I know? Children chatter so. I simply never pay any attention. It was just something to stick on a card. Instead of something about the weather. . . ."

Miss Emily ignored her, turning to Carol-Ann. "Get Don. Have him meet us at Judge Bo's. That child's a walking time bomb! We've got to protect her. Hurry!"

Without lost motion Carol-Ann scooped up the phone. She had seen, almost as quickly as Miss Emily, the threat that hung over little Dawn Mathieson, who had undoubtedly seen a murderer. And once the killer knew the child was back in town . . . She got through to Don, found her voice wouldn't work, took a deep breath and started over.

She spoke swiftly, coherently. "Dawn Mathieson's mother wrote the card. About someone Dawn saw in Charleston. The murderer must think she saw him, or he wouldn't have stolen the card. The child's at Judge Bo's. We'll meet you there." Don didn't need more. He understood.

"Murder!" Mildred Mathieson gasped. "Why didn't you tell me?"

"And scatter what wits you've got?"

"I'm not always a fool." She didn't look it then. She looked grim—and a little frightened. "My car's outside."

Carol-Ann ran beside Mildred. "Can you drive? Fast?"

"I drove an ambulance at Pearl Harbor." She already had a door open. "And Dawn's my child."

Carol-Ann didn't waste words. She leapt in behind Mrs. Mathieson and the car was in motion before she could sit down.

"Shortest route!" Mildred Mathieson barked it, and Miss Emily gave directions, swiftly, concisely. Then she sat back, massaging the head of her stick, her eyes bleak and unhappy.

"It's those murders." Mildred Mathieson flung the words over her shoulder, asking for information, helping to orient herself. "And you think Dawn saw something."

"Not necessarily. But the murderer does. Or why steal your card?"

"I heard about it. You were injured. Your head—"

"Not badly. Curlers saved me."

"Oh! Nobody mentioned curlers."

Miss Emily scowled, but Carol-Ann was sure it wasn't over the fact that her story had been slighted. It was something else. Something that had Miss Emily muttering under her breath. "Nobody mentioned curlers. Nobody mentioned curlers? And they should have. Curlers on a fat woman are funny. They make a good story. But nobody mentioned curlers. Why?" She snapped her ringed fingers.

"Because nobody knew about curlers—except Don, Cassie, Carol-Ann and the doctor. And the person who clobbered me. Nobody should have known about curlers. But somebody did. I remember." And remembering, Miss Emily sagged back in the seat, her rugged old face crumpling. "I've been a fool. A stupid, blind fool!" Her stick rapped on the back of the seat. "Faster!"

Carol-Ann, bracing herself in her corner, was remembering, too. A frail little man sitting primly in one of Miss Emily's needlepoint chairs, smiling and saying, "The curlers probably saved you from serious injury. At least those hideous things have some useful purpose."

Judge Bo!

Carol-Ann began putting bits and pieces together, bits and pieces that should have been put together long ago. The readiness of the lie about Ted's ten thousand, dollars. And how had he known it had once been ten thousand? The police had only known of nine thousand, up to that day. And his flimsy alibis. For Earps' murder, for instance—that he had smoked an extra cigar outside Miss Thalia's house. And if they had examined that one closely at the time they'd have known he was lying. He had said he had rung Miss Thalia's doorbell and she hadn't answered. But she hadn't left the house until after the crash—which followed the murder. So it had been later—some minutes later—that Judge Bo had rung the bell. The alibi was no good.

But vague, gentle Judge Bo! Then she remembered those brief flares of ferocity, like the time he had almost shot Jake. There were other things, too. He had known Miss Thalia's house well enough to slip in and steal the blue-and-gold robe—and he was small enough to have worn it. Those tiny, neat feet of his could have slid, shoes and all, into Jake's huge brogans—would have needed the padding of papers to hold them on. Another thing, he hadn't even threatened injury to either Miss Thalia or Carol-Ann on that surreptitious night visit. And on that one to Miss Emily's, he'd been almost absurdly gentle with his bashing.

The most horrible thing of all was what faced them. It had started with that absurd postcard—and now it would end with it. And little Dawn caught in between. What was it she had said? "Now I have to go over and help Judge Bo watch his ice-maker. I promised." And Dawn, in brief red trunks, had gone on to a real-life game of her childishly mispronounced Corpse and Robbers.

Couldn't Mildred drive any faster? Just as Carol-Ann leaned forward to urge more speed, they slewed wildly sideways, bounced over a ditch and careened toward a startlingly modern house that looked at them out of two narrow horizontal windows like squinting, curious eyes.

Miss Emily was out of the car, thudding across the newly sodded lawn with an awkward, lurching gait that nevertheless covered space. Mildred Mathieson was only a step behind her. Carol-Ann caught up with them just as Miss Emily unceremoniously burst open the front door and hurtled through. Mildred Mathieson shot after her and Carol-Ann came up behind them.

For a moment her eyes wouldn't adjust to the inside gloom. Then, abruptly, it wasn't gloom any more, but a cheerfully sunlit room, considerably longer than it was wide, with the pier of a Roman brick fireplace separating off what was probably a dining area. And against the fireplace, his arm resting negligently along the heavy, hand-hewn beam that served as a mantel, stood Judge Bo. He bowed slightly to each of them.

"Where is she?" Miss Emily asked huskily.

Judge Bo's arm swept off the mantel, and his thin, almost transparent hand pointed at them, holding one of his prized derringers.

"I didn't expect you quite so soon."

23

Judge Bo smiled almost shyly at them, holding the derringer perfectly steady. "You shouldn't have guessed so quick." His voice was sad, a little weary.

Mildred Mathieson walked slowly down the long room toward him, ignoring the gun. "Where is my child?"

"Please! Don't come any closer. You must see I can't let you—"

Mildred nodded almost reasonably toward the gun. "I recognize that. It's a derringer. It fires only one shot. Maybe you can kill me but the others will get you. Put it down and let me have my child. I don't care about the law. I'll even hold these others here while you get away." It was all so sane, so calm, so reasonable that Carol-Ann found herself almost daring to hope he'd believe her.

"Just give me the gun and I'll keep them here while you get away." So different from the silly, vaporous woman of a few minutes ago. "Let me have my child!"

"Child?" Judge Bo's eyes wavered from the woman to Miss Emily. "What child, Emily?"

Miss Emily clumped forward, shoving Mildred aside. "It's no use, Bo. I know she's here. And I know what she's done. You can't protect her forever, Bo."

The fragile old man by the fireplace began to shake. "Emily! Emily! I've tried—"

"A child's life is at stake, Bo. Little Dawn Mathieson."

A brief smile flickered on his tired old face. "Yes. Dawn. Charming child. She came to watch the ice-maker."

"Please!" Mildred Mathieson started forward but Miss Emily's huge arm blocked her.

"Dawn was in Charleston, Bo. She saw what happened on Ted's boat. So she's dangerous. And in danger."

"No!" Judge Bo glanced wildly down at the derringer in his hand as if he had discovered a cobra. "Oh, dear God, no! She promised to take her home. In my car."

"You know she never bothered to learn to drive—" Miss Emily disregarded the wavering derringer and hurtled on, past Judge Bo, across the dining room, toward the kitchen. Mildred hesitated only an instant, as if to regroup her wildly churning thoughts, and then spurted ahead, passing Miss Emily and charging through the swing door that obviously led to a kitchen.

Carol-Ann had that brief moment with Judge Bo. She saw his old face crumble inward, as if all that sustained it had been sucked away. He sagged against the mantel, burying his ravaged face in his arm. "Dear God, what have I done!"

Carol-Ann left him there, an old, broken man, and ran for the kitchen. It was empty, but another door opened on to a short flight of stairs leading down to a combination garage and utility room. She slid bumpily down three steps, into Miss Emily's broad back.

Mildred Mathieson was already several steps away, moving slowly, deliberately, almost mechanically, toward the far end of the room where Miss Thalia stood, her thin body pressed against the white mass of a huge home freezer, one skinny arm extended, her claw-like hand clamped around the mate to Judge Bo's derringer.

"Don't!" The derringer jerked to the violence of her speech.

"She's only a child." Mildred's voice held steady, except for the tiniest brittle crack. "Just a baby." She kept on walking.

Miss Thalia shook her head stubbornly. "I can't let her out. She'll tell."

Without turning her head Mildred spoke in a different tone, as if issuing orders. "Miss Emily, there's only one bullet. When she shoots, get to the box. Get Dawn out. Get—Dawn—out!"

Miss Thalia's head weaved on her thin neck, her prominent eyes bulging. "I can't let her out. You see that, don't you? She'll tell. She saw me in Charleston. So I can't let her—" Her pale, prominent eyes stretched even wider. The gun twitched. "Don't!" Her mouth opened in a nerve-shattering scream. "Don't!"

The gun thundered and roared in the small room, nearly deafening Carol-Ann, and heavy black powder fogged stingingly across her eyes.

In an instant it cleared and she could see.

Miss Thalia still stood there, but she no longer held the gun. Her arm drooped limply at her side and she was staring down at it in wild disbelief, as if she couldn't understand why it had failed her. Then her knees buckled with appalling slowness and she crumbled almost gently on the concrete floor.

Mildred Mathieson stepped over Miss Thalia's slight, crumpled figure and reached for the latch of the home freezer, lifting it tenderly as if she were afraid it might shatter. Sobbing, she leaned into the box and lifted out a small figure in brief red trunks, cradling it against her breast. "Baby, baby. . . ."

"Hi, Mommy." The voice was thin, weary almost to the point of exhaustion, but still a voice. "I don't think much of that game." Then the shivering started. Thin shaking arms went up and around Mildred's neck; a wide-eyed, freckled face muzzled against her neck. "I'm sleepy—"

"Get her out of here!" Miss Emily looked up from taking
the derringer out of Miss Thalia's nerveless fingers. "Wrap
her up warm. Bo's got blankets."

Carol-Ann had to lead Mildred up the steps and into
the house, find the blankets, and then pry the child out of
her arms. Then the two of them were rubbing the thin little arms and legs, massaging the cold back, rubbing briskly
with towels. At last Dawn opened her eyes, sighing deeply.
She smiled at her mother. "Hi, Mommy."

Judge Bo was kneeling beside Miss Thalia, cradling her
head in his arms, his tired old eyes studying her face.
"Forgive me, Thalia, but I couldn't let you kill anybody
else. Not that child."

Miss Thalia's prominent eyes scanned his face, then
she glanced stealthily around. "But I couldn't let her out.
She'd tell. She saw me in Charleston, you know, when I
went to see Ted. But he wouldn't give me the money back,
and I had to return it. You do understand, don't you, Bo?
I couldn't let him sell dear Father's name." She pursed
her lips against the pain of memory. "Why, do you know,
he was going to let that Scudder person have the rights
to the land dear Father gave the city. But I couldn't let
him. Father gave that land—nobly, unselfishly, out of the
greatness of his heart. But Ted just laughed. He said dear
Father always meant to take it back and deliberately made
out the papers wrong. So I took—"

"Oh, no!"

"I knew you'd see it my way, Bo. But Ted . . ." She
coughed faintly. "Ted said now everybody would know
what a hypocrite and scoundrel Father was. Those were
his very words, Bo. Hypocrite and scoundrel. And then
he laughed. That's when I hit him. I didn't mean to hit
so hard, but I had to get the money to give back to that
awful Scudder person." She shuddered and lay quiet for

a long moment, then she stirred restlessly in Judge Bo's arms. "Oh, dear! I can't lie here. What will people think? I must get up!"

"Lie still, Thalia. You're hurt. The ambulance will be here in a moment."

Thalia sighed and relaxed. "I don't really hurt. I'm just tired, Bo. Awfully tired. I've been doing too much. Dear Father always said, 'Conserve your strength'—but I couldn't. That awful Scudder person was going to use Father's land—" She seemed to gather strength for a disdainful sniff—"for an amusement park."

"Oh, he couldn't!"

"Yes he could, Bo. Dear Father wasn't very practical, you know. He was such a dreamer. So the papers were made out wrong. And Ted really could get the land back and sell it to the Scudder person. And everybody would have thought dear Father was a fool—or maybe even a crook. I couldn't let that happen, just when the town he founded had decided to put up a Memorial, could I? So I took the money back to that Scudder person." She shuddered once and slumped against Judge Bo's frail chest.

He looked up in mute appeal at Miss Emily's face.

"Let her talk, Bo. It can't hurt anything."

He sighed and looked down at the thin, wasted caricature of the woman he had loved for so many years.

"Yes, Bo? Oh, I was telling you about that Scudder person, wasn't I? He was awful. Simply horrible. I even put on the prettiest robe I could find. Blue-and-gold. You always said I looked nice in blue. And I gave him the money back, but he said it was a thousand dollars short and he didn't want it anyway after I'd welched on my bargain. His very words. Welched! As if I'd ever have agreed to make that creature of his Madam Chairman—a woman like that, representing Father's Memorial."

"But, dear, you did agree."

"Not you, too, Bo! I only agreed to it when he threatened to put up that amusement park. But once I took the
money back from Ted, I didn't think . . . Well, with Ted
gone, I certainly expected him to take the money back.
You do think he should have taken it, don't you? But he
wouldn't. He said after what I did to that—that woman of
his—I should be glad if he only made Father out a fool,
instead of proving he was a crook. Yes, he said that, Bo.
Father—a crook. And when—when I offered him . . ."
Miss Thalia whimpered painfully. "He laughed. Such horrid laughter, Bo. So I just stuck the knife in him. It was
Emily's best bone-handled knife, which made it worse."

Very gently, at a nod from Don, Judge Bo prodded her
again into talking. "What about Willie? You know—Willie
Earps."

"You heard him. Nasty little man, whispering to me
that day at the courthouse. He said he knew who stabbed
that Scudder person. And he was going to tell. And he
knew about Father, too, and the mistake he made. So you
can see I had to stop him." She made a feeble gesture toward him, smiling naughtily. "You almost caught me that
time, didn't you? Coming to see me early. Impatient boy!"

Judge Bo pleaded again with his eyes to be allowed to
stop this thing, but both Don and Miss Emily shook their
heads in curiously synchronized rhythm. He bent once
more over Miss Thalia. "And that Andy Stevens?"

A fatuous smile touched Miss Thalia's gaunt face. "I
was clever there, wasn't I? Everybody thought he did those
things, so I just sneaked one of Ted's guns and went down
there and shot him. Through the window. And dropped the
gun inside. And it was all over. And dear Father's memory
was safe. He was a wonderful man, Bo. A truly wonderful
man. . . . All over. All over!" She sighed. "Until that child
came back. She saw me in Charleston. But I told you that,
didn't I? Her mother wrote me a post card. Stupid woman.

I couldn't make it out, though. Then Emily got one, too, and she's so clever at figuring things, I had to take hers. I hit her." Miss Thalia tinkled with old, brittle laughter. "Clank."

Her eyes went wide, focusing on Bo's face. "I didn't kill her, too, did I? I don't remember. Things don't seem clear. Am I dying, Bo? Am I? What happened to me? Oh, I remember. You shot me!" She strained to look at him, brows knit in faint surprise. "Why did you shoot me, Bo? What did I do?" She went limp in his arms, sighing.

Judge Bo wept.

Two days later they were seated in Miss Emily's living room, munching on one of Cassie's little snacks. Cynthia, Luke, Don, Carol-Ann and, of course, Miss Emily, who was regarding a large piece of fudge cake and weighing its merits against its calories. Merits won. She bit into the fudge cake, her eyes on Luke.

"Could Jake have taken away the land Judge Marsten gave the city?"

Luke scanned a platter of sandwiches carefully, selected one and sat back. "It wasn't a true gift. It had the element of rent—quite possibly intended to be perpetual. And frankly, the document Marsten drew up, deeding the city that land, was full of holes. Courts have ruled on lesser errors than he made. It was the work of an incompetent—or a crook."

"Judge Marsten wasn't smart enough to be a crook."

"Jake could have made reversion look intentional—and that would have made Marsten a crook. I fought him on that."

"Thanks. The town appreciates it."

"To be quite frank, I didn't do it for the town. I fought it on Jake's account—and mine. Such action would have precipitated suits that could have cost a fortune. I didn't think it was worth it. But Jake had his dander up. After that affair at the Memorial Party."

"So Thalia precipitated the very thing she feared?"

"She had already killed her brother. In Charleston," Luke reminded her. "And sailed his boat up to Albemarle Sound before she abandoned it. Probably caught a ride back to the Beach."

"Took a bus," Don corrected. "It's taken time, but we checked on it. She didn't even really try to cover up."

Miss Emily nodded sagely around the last of the fudge cake. "Not even with Jake's footprints. She wasn't covering up—just trying to confuse things. Like a child. I should have realized that very night that she had made the footprints herself. The cook book," she finished cryptically, licking the fudge off her fingertips.

"Cook book?" Carol-Ann wasn't sure she had heard correctly and rather hoped she hadn't. Then she remembered. "She had it in her hand when she was up on the sideboard. . . ."

Miss Emily nodded confirmation. "But she said she came from the living room. Where the light switch is. And I should have known that Thalia, as prim a housekeeper as she is, would never have left a cook book in the living room. I should have known, too, that she would never have crossed that whole room to get to the sideboard if an intruder had been anywhere near the window. She'd have had to pass right by him."

"But the cook book?"

"Weapon. A heavy book would be Thalia's idea of a weapon. She must have slipped out of Jake's shoes and scurried out the back door to hide them. Earps was undoubtedly watching and picked them up as evidence for blackmail. He must have started blackmailing her the very next day, as soon as he was sure of Jake's murder. After hiding the shoes, she came back in through the kitchen, picked up her 'weapon,' climbed on the sideboard and screamed."

Carol-Ann found it hard to believe. "You mean she staged it all?"

Miss Emily nodded. "And rather childishly. She was childish, you know. Judge Marsten never let her grow up. She looked inquiringly at Don. "How is she?"

"Very happy. She has plenty of blocks and spends all day building memorials."

The doorbell rang. Don sprang up to answer it and ushered in Judge Bo, sportily attired. He bowed charmingly. "I've been driving. Ronnie took me out with Betty Lou." A sweepingly gallant gesture invited them to the window to look. "Isn't she a beauty? Lovely. Lovely."

Carol-Ann made herself be the last to reach the window, determined not to exclaim over this hussy Ronnie insisted on flaunting. But there was only Ronnie sitting alone in a low, sleek sports car of unfamiliar design.

"That's Betty Lou. Ronnie's own design. We'll build them right here at Virginia Beach. Just the bodies, of course. For standard chassis."

Ronnie waved, slid over the low door and trotted up the walk. He came into the room, beaming. "What do you think of Betty Lou?" He took Carol-Ann's arm and walked her out on the porch. "We're already got orders for twenty. Made of fiberglass and plastic. Like to take a spin? My partner, the Judge, won't mind." He grinned. "He thinks they're made to take out pretty girls."

Carol-Ann peered over her shoulder at Don glowering from the doorway and decided maybe a little competition wouldn't hurt. She felt Ronnie's hand tighten on her arm, guiding her toward the steps.

Beside her Judge Bo was looking wistfully at the sleek sports car before he turned back to speak to Miss Emily.

"Thalia didn't realize what she was doing."

"No, she didn't, Bo. Not even when she asked you to claim Ted's missing money had been a commission from you."

Judge Bo looked surprised. "You knew? I didn't mean to deceive you, but Thalia hinted Ted had gotten the money dishonestly, so to save her the disgrace—"

"She just made up stories, Bo. That's probably why she got by with so much. Just sheer, muddling accident. She was like a child, pretending." Miss Emily listened to a rising shout around the corner of the house and saw a diminutive figure in a minuscule pair of red trunks scoot around the forsythia bush, a plastic six-shooter mowing down desperadoes. Miss Emily sighed. "She was like a child playing Corpse and Robbers."

THE AUTHORS

Douglas Stapleton was born Samuel Granville Staples (1907-1972) and grew up in Virginia. Douglas Stapleton may have started out as a pen-name, but appears to have been taken on for most professional use. According to one newspaper article, Stapleton "started out as a song-and-dance man with Eleanor Powell in her first success, 'The Wedding of the Painted Doll,' became historical correlator for the *Encyclopedia Britannica*, advertising man with General Foods, program manager for a radio station and radio commentator and (in Washington) administrator for the W.P.A. and later Radio Expert for the executive office of the president." After service in the naval reserve and teaching at the Ft. Monmouth signal corps O.C.S., he worked as an advertising executive in New York for a wide variety of TV and radio programs. As an author, Stapleton wrote a multitude of books, articles, short stories, radio plays, and television comedies.

It was while working in New York that he met and married his third (?) wife, Dorothy, in 1941. Dorothy Tucker Aden (1917-1970) was from Bastrop, Louisiana, where she had worked as a political speechwriter, theatrical company press agent, licensed engineer, radio station operator, film director and producer, and creator and writer for the army radio serial, 'This is Your Judge Advocate.'

Douglas and Dorothy Stapleton

She moved to New York to become director of radio, TV
and films for Grey Advertising, where she met Douglas.
While on their honeymoon, they co-produced a Broadway
play, 'Questionable Ladies,' and wrote their first novel together, *The Corpse is Indignant*. For that mystery Dorothy
used the pen-name Helen A. Carey. In future collabora-
tions, the pair went by Douglas and Dorothy Stapleton.
They continued to work together on radio shows, monthly
magazine columns, and other projects. *American Magazine*
called them "the people who work 48 hours a day." (For
relaxation, they both obtained their pilot's licenses.) They
'retired' to Virginia Beach in 1951, becoming involved
in community work and some further mystery writing for
Arcadia House (*Late for the Funeral, Corpse and Robbers,*
and *The Crime, the Place, and the Girl*). This retirement
didn't last long, as they had moved to Monroe, Louisiana,
in 1953 to help operate a new radio station, though it shut
down the next year. Their mystery novel writing ended
after the mid-1950s (though short stories for mystery and
science fiction magazines were published into the 1960s),
and they appear to have lived their final years in Los
Angeles, California.

A JUDGE MASSIE MYSTERY

THE CORPSE IS INDIGNANT

DOUGLAS STAPLETON
and HELEN A. CAREY

Details at
CoachwhipBooks.com

Available from your favorite online retailers

THE QUINNY HITE
MYSTERIES

CHINESE RED · HERE LIES THE BODY

RICHARD BURKE

THE SERGEANT HARTY MYSTERIES

JOEL Y. DANE

MURDER CUM LAUDE

1

THE CABANA MURDERS

Details at
CoachwhipBooks.com

Available from your favorite online retailers

Drink the Green Water
The Milkmaid's Millions

HUGH AUSTIN

Details at
CoachwhipBooks.com

Available from your favorite online retailers

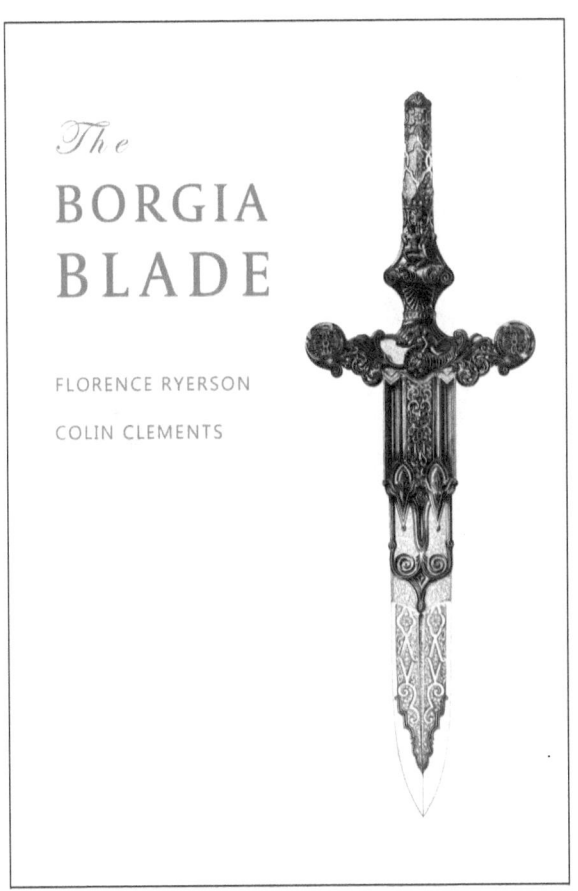

THERE IS
NO RETURN
THE ADELAIDE ADAMS MYSTERIES
ANITA BLACKMON

Details at
CoachwhipBooks.com

Available from your favorite online retailers

FULL CRASH DIVE

ALLAN R. BOSWORTH

Details at
CoachwhipBooks.com

Available from your favorite online retailers